The Sin Eater

and other stories

The Sin Eater

and other stories

Elizabeth Frankie Rollins

Queen's Ferry Press

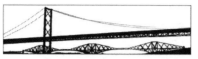

Queen's Ferry Press
8240 Preston Road
Suite 125-151
Plano, TX 75024
www.queensferrypress.com

Copyright © 2013 by Elizabeth Frankie Rollins

Published 2013 by Queen's Ferry Press

Cover design by Ben Johnson & Noah Saterstrom
Interior images by Ben Johnson

First edition February 2013

ISBN 978-1-938466-05-2

Printed in the United States of America

Praise for *The Sin Eater and Other Stories*:

"The way the human condition—with all its difficult, marvelous details: solitude, interruptions, loves—is constellated in these stories by Elizabeth Frankie Rollins reframes the vast space between ourselves and others. Where seemingly there is nothing in the spaces between, here we read *compassion through attention*. This book performs its title, visits us like a Sin Eater in the night, so that we all might learn better how to rest in peace even as we live with all of our messy love, hope, and desire."

—Selah Saterstrom, author of *The Meat and Spirit Plan*

"A few years ago I heard Elizabeth Rollins present 'The New Plague' at a reading. I thought back then that it was the best story I had heard in a long, long time. Rereading it, I still think it is one of the best stories *ever*. And I am happy to report that the rest of this book is pretty darn awesome. Rollins has vision, voice, and heart, and an ear for what disturbs and what restores us. Anyone with an interest in what's really going on in new American fiction should read her work."

—Rebecca Brown, author of *American Romances*

"In this brilliant and riveting collection of stories Frankie Rollins provides a courageous and intimate glimpse of the human psyche in distress. We are magnetized to plague, secret anatomy, and the allure of inexplicable impulses which blur reality with the uncanny. In *The Sin Eater and Other Stories* we encounter a haunting text which lingers on the tongue, and an adept talent in the tradition of the best of storytellers—which strikes the reader as both new and yet reassuringly familiar—a voice one is immediately compelled to trust."

—Laynie Browne, author of *Roseate Points of Gold*

"Rollins' first collection places her solidly in the company of writers such as Aimee Bender, Kevin Brockmeier, and Deborah Eisenberg. The trapdoors in her stories are impeccably placed. Rollins knows all too well the beautiful, dangerous, bewildering human heart, and her stories live in the lulls between its beats."

—Roy Kesey, author of *Pacazo* and *All Over*

"*The Sin Eater* consumed me night after night, enchanting me with its shape-shifting tales. This debut collection from spellbinder and fairy-tale marvel Elizabeth Frankie Rollins is a prophetic and wonderful book."

—Kate Bernheimer, author of *Horse, Flower, Bird*

"Elizabeth Frankie Rollins has drawn back the bowstring of apocalypse and let her arrow tales fly—a terrific debut collection that always hits its mark."

—Brent Hendricks, author of *A Long Day at the End of the World*

For the Corvids

Table of Contents

The New Plague

T he cat was a runt, small and gray, her head cocked in such a way that she reminded me of an old Spanish lady wearing a lace mantilla. I would open the back door and wherever she was, somewhere down in the creek among broken glass and tires and plastic bags, she'd hear me and come running. She'd run across the stubby grass, her pink mouth mewing, and I couldn't help myself. I'd go back inside for tuna and a bowl of fresh water.

Chas didn't like that cat. He has always feared unknown things, dangers that lurk in his mother's warnings. Parasites on birds, rabid squirrels, germs on doorknobs, public bathrooms. He is afraid of food prepared by neighbors, public swimming pools and, of course, stray dogs and cats. Besides these, the plague we'd been reading about that had come to a neighboring town.

Turns out he was right to dislike the cat, but I've always

rejected that kind of blanket fear. The little crooked-headed cat ran across the lawn to me, and I fed her, and when she was finished, I picked her up and held her tiny body. I felt her flimsy, bony life and got her rumble-purr going, and it made me happy. She needed love and I gave it to her. It's about love, I told Chas, the oldest reciprocal relationship on Earth. He gave me a look and said, "I guess you don't count parasites." No, I told him, parasites aren't reciprocal.

Chas showed the first symptom. A swelling on his inner thigh. A fat, tender welt like a beetle wedged under his skin.

They tell us the plague has, over time, changed drastically. This is a new strain. We won't die in three to seven days, but we will die sooner than most. And until then, quarantine.

The Spanish lady still comes to the yard, but the back door is now sealed against exit or entry with the thick plastic sheeting that covers the whole house. I thought she would be afraid of the huge, noisy generator that pumps air inside, but she isn't. She cases the lawn, looking for me, and I can see her calling, little pink mouth opening and shutting in the silence of that monstrous roar.

Since our discharge from the hospital and our journey home in the white quarantine van, we haven't spoken to anyone face-to-face but each other. It's no longer possible. We can use the telephone and computer, of course, but no more lunches or dinners with friends. No work at the office. No traveling for holidays. No coffee shops, or shops of any kind. You won't find us on the streets or in a drugstore or at a bar. We have already ceased—in many ways—to exist.

In the quarantine van, its air tainted and chemical, we wore the silver suits, which stank of new plastic and made sweat pour from our armpits. Neon-green plague lights on the van's roof reflected off the houses we passed and circled around to move across our faces. In the hospital they told us that we were the second house in our development to be infected. Disease was swifter in the first home, though, as we've already outlived that entire family.

We received phone calls, but no one knew what to say—least of all us. We gave the update, and then they called back for a new update. Some days, I'd repeat myself five times before giving up answering the phone altogether. I left a message on the answering machine that said we don't have any news. The machine filled and then people stopped calling, even our family members. Now we don't talk to anyone.

In medieval times, we'd be long dead. Covered in beetle bulges and patches of liver-and-blackened skin, coughing up black blood. We would be ancient in our disfigurement.

In the hospital, we were as docile as doll babies. We let them jab and swab and test and console and wrap and unwrap us. Doctors asked us cheerful questions and serious questions, and we lay quiet in all the noise, that din, those lights too bright. We were stunned into submission. We went limp and weak. It was behavior antithetical to our professions, our years of training, our years of adulthood. In the care of the staff, we became children who had gotten themselves into trouble and required rescue. We let them hold in their palms everything we were.

They tell us we might not die. They tell us cures come along every day, but I don't believe they can cure this. They merely trick it away, trick it into remission. A disease can be tricked, but in truth, it's the natural trickster. It always finds its way back. No matter how far civilization progresses, the old channels remain open.

We have charts that the doctors made for us, a step-by-step prognosis of the disease's path through the body. Chas, of course, has already experienced the bubo, and it wasn't until we were in the hospital that an ulcerated flea bite on my ankle was discovered. That day the nurse said to me, "You have a bite just above your medial malleolus." I told her I didn't know what she meant and she sighed impatiently. "Means you're infected," she said.

A series of stages is supposed to occur. A host of buboes on the groin, neck, and thighs; fever; the lungs filling; then chills; delirium; the skin in rosy continents burning to black.

The house is fumigated now, every plant dead as testament. Chas is angry with me, though he won't come out and say as much. He shares his dreams over carrot juice in the mornings and tells me in them I am always reassuring him that the snake wrapped round his chest is harmless, the murderer with a knife at his throat is a man who means well, and so on. In the study he watches endless television. His conversation has started to reference all the shows and movies he sees. Sometimes when we eat together, he'll recite a line from a movie rather than reply to a question I've asked. We're not used to spending so much time together. It's hard to tell if we're ignoring each other on purpose or if, when you're both always at home, it's natural to pass in the hall without speaking, nodding like coworkers. It's as though we're becoming characters in blue screen, flickering in and out of snow.

Occasionally, Chas will mention what's happening with the plague out in the world, but it's begun to sound like the repetition you hear during snowstorms: the number of inches, the texture of the accumulation, repeated again and again. They describe the history of plague, where it began in modernity, the symptoms, the death toll—which is pretty high. One night Chas came to bed and when I asked him what he'd been watching, he said, "They're dying like flies out there," and then he picked up a book and started to read.

Money rolls in from both our jobs. Disability insurance and plague insurance, things we scorned, but bought, as professional people tend to do. Now we have lots of money in our account, but nothing to spend it on. Chas told me that people without money and insurance are being treated en masse in covered stadiums, schools, and government buildings. Whole towns have been quarantined. Most of New Mexico and Arizona, some of Ohio.

We've read the New Plague web pages, taken the interactive tests on-line, listened to the physicians in the hospital who dispensed theories from the plexiglass entrance to our room. The more we try to investigate, the fewer conclusions we reach. The disease has been around forever, and the global disease centers tracked it, but there's no indication that anyone expected it to come back like this, so vigorous and rabid.

There's a whole section of the prognosis we can't even decipher. In the newer texts on the subject, there is repeated mention of a Visitor. It reads like this: *An entity which comes to the house, to the plague-infected.* Is it a doctor? A specialist? Is it even a person? Occasionally, we'll read something that implies the Visitor is a representative of the disease itself. What could that mean? When we ask the doctors, they smile nervously and change the subject. One doctor tells me, "You can only learn so much at a time. There's only so much capacity for dread."

Dread? We are dying. Is there anything more to dread?

Eventually we learn that there's not much information about the Visitor because everyone who has actually received a Visit is dead. That's what we read, finally, in a cutting-edge on-line medical journal. There's a bunch of information about the alkaline and acidic properties of "traces" left behind, and the flat statement that no one survives a Visit.

It's bizarre, so voodoo and tea leaf, so unlike anything having to do with the hospital, with its heaps of paperwork and billings and insurance referrals and sterilized needles and bottles of unpronounceable chemicals, that I can't even begin to grasp the notion. I read the older texts about the medieval plague, about the charnel houses, pest houses, death carts, but there's no mention of the Visitor. The Visitor is new.

One night I dream of the Visitor. It is bent over Chas. The hunched back is a lumpy, shiny, seeping mass. The whole body looks once-human but now pus-filled, bruised, visibly burning with illness. As I watch, it touches Chas with a charred stump and his skin begins to bubble, giving off a wet, boiling noise. When I wake I'm hyperventilating.

We await the Visitor with dread, more dread.

The charts fascinate me. They're intricate maps of our actual body scans, marked with the various episodic phases of the disease. The day they gave them to us I marveled; they looked like something else, something artful. There's a loveliness to the color choices, the ways in which disease is slowly shaded into various organs, the cloying, definitive black lines of dying tissue.

The doctors told us that if the cat had never come inside the house, we might have escaped infection.

Chas came home from work one night as I was roasting a chicken, sipping from a glass of wine. I had the jazz station on the radio, the house was clean, and I was happy. I'd let the cat in, and she had settled into Chas' favorite chair. When she had come to the door, her head cocked to the side like a question, I couldn't say no.

I'm not like him. I don't like living by the limits of warnings, even well-meant ones. I don't want a prophylactic life. I act on whim. I'm spontaneous. That day, it seemed as though the cat was meant to come in. She and I had some kind of thing, a friendship, and I believe in honoring friendships. I just forgot about the plague that day. I did. It still seemed so far-fetched. I hadn't seen the plague vans yet, or read about the disease reaching our town, and I clean forgot about it.

Of course, it looks like that was the night we were infected.

Now that the house is wrapped in plastic and everything we own, including our bodies, is sterilized to the nth degree, I wonder if I had it to do over, would I still let the cat in? I probably would. In fact, I worry about her terribly, but she hasn't come around in days. The doctors say she's certain to be dead.

Sometimes I look down at my hands and I see them turning the lock, opening the door, reaching for her tiny, light body. I see them holding her, lifting her to my mouth, kissing her head, her tail curling around my arm for balance. The gestures of these hands, their movements and shape and heat, these things will be gone soon. There will be nothing left of them, no mark, this life I've lived nothing more than a breeze, a long exhalation.

Every afternoon there's a drop of foods and meds and books and gifts. These are delivered just outside our front door to a self-sanitizing box. Some of the things we find in our daily drop are shocking. They're mass-producing casseroles for the sick. Each one comes with a preprinted *To* and *From* tag with "Get Well" scrawled in fancy script across the top. Specially defined ingredients, according to your disease. On the outside of the boxes, there are little squares to check for Plague, Aids, Cancer, Sexually Transmitted Disease, Addiction, Heart Disease, and so on. The plague-infected get casseroles of rice and carrot and raisin, held together by some sticky, unidentifiable brown sauce. We get cookies, too. The cookies are also ingredient-specific. Plague cookies are oatmeal raisin. We got a box of the sexually transmitted by accident once, and when we tasted the cookies, they were sugarless lumps of dough.

Your diet becomes severely restricted at the onset of plague, so much so that they limit your on-line food-ordering capability. One night, trying to make up with Chas, I get my friend Nancy to drop some takeout Chinese into our box. I know she is brave enough to come, but she hesitates, wondering if it isn't bad for us. I say, Nancy, are you going to let me die without one last spring roll? I am joking, of course, and it is the first time I realize that I know nothing about expecting to die. Shouldn't something have shifted, other than an intensification of dread?

I load the table with all that glorious food from Elena Wu's and when Chas comes in, he mock swoons just from the smell. We have spring rolls and dim sum and the sauces, four different main dishes, and a separate bag of fortune cookies. Nancy stuck a note in with fake Chinese writing, which she translated into *Bon Appetit!* I show Chas and he laughs and reaches out and runs his fingers over my forearm, light and loving. It is the first night I think he might still love me, even after what I've done.

The last time I sent in the food order on the computer, I also sent along an order for craft store items: Styrofoam balls and feathers and beads and fabrics and wire and string and glue and putty and, on a whim, a deck of playing cards. I don't know what I'm going to do with it all, but I feel excited about it, and that seems like something.

Every second day we draw each other's blood into tubes for the doctors to pick up. Last time we spoke with them on the phone, we overheard a voice in the background say, Jesus, those two are still alive?

The diffused light that the plastic allows through our windows has a quality that leaves me thirsty. I crave daylight, hard branches, angled roofs, clotheslines. I check every window, including the basement and tiny attic ones, to see if there might be a crack, a sliver somewhere of real, crisp vision. There is none. Some days, I stare so hard through the plastic that my eyes are blurry for a long time after. Our house has gone internal, milk-lit, and loud as a womb.

Chas sleeps horribly late into the day and sometimes when I'm wandering the house I see him flung across the bed with his mouth open. I stop and stare and the feelings that surge through me are too complicated to understand. His face, that mouth, oh, that familiar mouth. And then frustration at the sprawl, that insouciant sprawl, indifferent to all the years we're losing.

Sometimes I feel like I am going to be sick. I bend at the waist and wait for the nausea to rise or subside. I think of our deaths, how we will convulse and heave and writhe, blistered and violently textbook-ill.

Two weeks have passed since we got home from the hospital, and I've started a life-sized version of my chart. I nail an old canvas tarp to some pine lengths we had originally bought for a compost bin; it makes a pretty good canvas. I do the buboes in shiny red sequins, glued onto plastic egg halves. They are mounded, vaguely sexual and disturbing. The arteries are in pulled indigo yarn but most veins are in colored wire. Organs are in a variety of textured fabrics, satin and silk and brocade markings of disease. I make the heart out of a red feather boa, which is a stunning touch. It looks—when a current of air hits it—like it is beating.

The re-invention of one's own organs gives a sense of life lived. You wonder at the rise and fall of those organs, as if you could remember when they were new and whole. One day I get the idea to do an entire series of these charts, in different colors and materials, to represent different times in life. Childhood, teenage years, early marriage. The year my mother died. How would you physically represent sorrow? Maybe a sexual version, too. I get out a pad of paper and begin making notes for different versions, how I'll let the materials speak for the time line, or colors for mood. I'm thrilled, but it could be delirium. It feels like I'm smiling. I touch my face.

When I look up, Chas is in the room. "Jesus Christ," he says, staring at the bowls of paint and glue and feather bits and scraps of material all over the room. The way he said *Jesus Christ*, in just that way, something scornful and hard at the center of it, sounding just like his father, makes me stand up in the midst of my stuff.

"What?" I cross my arms over my chest.

"What are you doing in here?"

"I'm making something."

"Why?" His disbelief is palpable.

"*Why?* Why not?"

He raises his eyebrows sarcastically, and just then, for the first time, he looks ugly to me. "Jesus Christ. We're dying. Don't you get it? We're *dying* right now."

"So?" I've picked up a twist of wire, and I drop it, suddenly embarrassed. It's the way he talks to people he doesn't respect, that condescending tone.

"What's the fucking point?" He continues. "It's not like you're going to finish. Are you hoping to be the first plague artist? Create an artwork of the doomed, the Aids quilt?"

My mouth falls open a little, almost comically, and I feel a blush burning across my cheeks. He has never spoken to me like this before. I hate him for it. Finally I say, "This is personal, asshole. Just because you're glued to the TV all day doesn't mean somebody else in this house isn't still interested in living."

"Oh yeah?" And a look comes over his face, and I know he's going to say it, and then he says it: "Well, I'm not the one who let the goddamned cat in the house."

He leaves the room. I don't blame him for leaving. I want him to leave. There is nothing else to say. It is a relief, of sorts, to have it said, to have him accuse me.

But the deeper, more pitiful truth is that I had pictured him coming in and being surprised, maybe amazed by my work. As if my new project, at the expense of his life, was something to celebrate.

I wish I'd let the cat in by accident, but I didn't. I meant to let her in. I wanted to let her in. I wasn't afraid, and this is what happens. I'm a foolish woman.

I look at the face I've designed for my life-sized chart. I've used the queen of spades as a model. When you hold all the queens, she's the one facing away from the others. She has a bad reputation. I touch the beading I've added to her headdress. She's treacherous, selfish, coquettish. You can see it all over her face.

Chas comes back in around three in the afternoon, his face stricken.

I sit back on my heels.

"I just saw the cat," he says. "In the backyard."

We call the doctors. Within a half-hour the yard is filled with men in quarantine suits. Chas and I pull up stools to the sliding glass doors and peer out through the thick plastic. It must seem kind of sad, that we enjoy it so much, but we sit there and I wave at anyone who looks up. People! We can't quite make them out, since they're in the suits and we're looking through plastic, but it's the most live action we've seen, and we're addicted. One guy stands and stares at us after I wave, as if we've startled him—like dead things reanimated.

They search until dusk and then they pack up and leave. I know it is bad news that they can't find the cat, that if they could find her, they'd be able to tell us more about why we are still alive, or when we'll die, but I'm glad they don't. I don't want her to be deprived of her shadowy walks in the bushes, her stretches in the sun. I don't want her to be locked in a cage, cut apart cell by cell, every hair a measure of cold research.

Once the searchers leave, Chas disappears into the cellar and brings up a bottle of wine. I find a pound of homemade pasta in the freezer, and we eat noodles with garlic and oil, and drink wine. The stimulation of seeing other people has inspired us, or the fight has cleared the air. We talk more than we have in weeks. I feel as though I'm seeing his face again, the way I used to, with adoration.

Afterwards, we end up sitting on the steps in the front hall and talking a little more, about what it was like before the disease. I half expect him to get up and go watch television, or suggest we watch a movie, but he doesn't. He seems content to sit talking with me.

After a while, he says, "You know what I realized while we were watching those guys?"

"No," I say.

"That bubo is gone. Completely gone. Healed with nothing left but a scar."

We rise at the same time and hurry into the room where I have the charts. They clearly indicate the buboes' growth, the swelling until bursting, their multiplication, the takeover they exert on the body. We stare at each other.

Chas asks, "Do you think we might not die?"

"Well," I lower my voice as if delivering bad news. "Eventually we will."

"Oh, well, yeah," Chas says, and we start laughing. Then I bend over the life-size chart and he leans and looks at it, too, touching the boa heart admiringly.

"This is actually really cool," he says.

I look at his hand, reaching out and touching the heart, and suddenly I'm flushed and hot and full of everything we've lost.

"I'm sorry. It's my fault," I whisper. "I know it. There's no way for you to forgive me, but I didn't, I didn't mean . . ." The heat of guilt surges, a scorching grief. I think about how I loathe the frivolous, treacherous face I see every day in the mirror. I can feel the terrible cracking of my sobs against the silence of the room and his warm hands touching me, soothing me, and it's all so relentless and final and desperate.

He leads me back to the stairs as I begin to calm, my face soaked, tissues clutched in wads, and he puts his arm around me and lowers me to the step. He looks at me and says, "Annie, I don't really blame you. It's not you. I know that. Look at the TV. It's everywhere. It's not you. I was just jealous, I think. That you were doing something in that room. That you have so much courage."

I start tearing up again and say, "But I let the cat in."

"Jesus, Annie. It's not like that. That's not the way it is. I shouldn't have said that." He peers into my face and I can see he forgives me, and then I know it's I who cannot forgive myself.

After a while, I say, "I wish we would hurry up and die, Chas. Or that we were already dead. Or that we weren't going to die knowing it. I wish we were going to die spontaneously, like other people." He looks at me as though I've said something strange.

I hear a pleading enter my voice: "Maybe we don't have to die now, like they say we will. Maybe we could live a new life. What if this is just one in a series, and not the only one?"

He looks at me, hard, intent, and then he smiles. Electrified, I feel both of us sitting on those steps, as alive as we can be, as though we've just become flesh again, our bodies turned whole, pulses resumed, breaths exhaled, the effort dampening our skin.

"Annie," he says, smiling. "Are you crazy? A whole series of lives? Does anyone want that?"

I'm exhausted, like I was after the first day in the hospital. I slump against the stairs. "I want to go out in the front yard and watch fireflies."

"Let's go to bed," says Chas, and there is tenderness as he takes me to bed and holds me.

In the middle of the night, the Visitor comes. We hear the plastic sheets rustling, then the front door—which hasn't been touched in weeks—clicks open. Almost immediately we smell it, breathing deeply at the same moment. Chas pulls the flashlight from the drawer and we creep to the stairs. Here we encounter the fresh air hugely and we stand, dragging it into our lungs, greedy, and then we gag, for another scent is also on the air, brutal and sharp. We hear the sound, an open mouth struggling for breath, a clotted, messy gulping. The Visitor is in the kitchen, knocking things over. We hear wet, sticky-sounding grunts. Chas aims the flashlight on the living room, *ready*, and when we hear the noise move, the ragged, sloppy breathing, he snaps it on. The Visitor turns toward the light and we freeze. The Visitor lifts its terrible face and sniffs us, deeply, wetly. Before Chas snaps off the light, I see the engorged and misshapen skull, the disintegrating arms, the legs, still upright, though molting skin and effluvia roll in a mass down the exposed bones. Chas lifts me off the stairs and staggering, clawing at each other hysterically, we flee to our bedroom, lock the door, and hide together in the closet, in the dark.

We tremble in silence for hours, hearing nothing. Occasionally we look at each other. I can make out his hair, and the dim lines of his face and shoulders. I can hear his breathing. We hold hands. We hear nothing, still.

We awake early, curled amid shoes and fallen hangers. Chas is using a sweater as a pillow. I have been sleeping against his thigh. When we see each other, we raise our eyebrows, and Chas leads us out of the closet and into the bedroom, which is as we left it. We head downstairs.

There is a mottled, white-and-rust-colored line from the living room, a crusted trail, from the spot where we'd seen the Visitor, to the door. We call the doctors. They arrive in ten minutes in their quarantine suits. They kneel and take samples, and the whole time they whisper to one another and keep an eye on us. We sit on the stairs again. There is an excited, carnival air to the proceedings. They draw our blood and take fragments of our hair and fingernails. They look at Chas' vanished bubo and my healed bite. They give us silver suits to wear and resterilize the house.

They ask us to join them in the kitchen. They smile thinly at us from inside their suits, three doctors we've dealt with before. I stare at their specifics through the face shields: watery brown eyes, yellowing buckteeth, a silvery beard running together in my mind. I'd forgotten that human faces were so vivid and individual and colorful.

"We don't understand," one of them says.

"Understand what?" asks Chas.

They chuckle shyly, looking at one another and then at the table. The silver-beard one fiddles with the Velcro on the sleeve of his suit. The bucktooth doctor says, "You both should be dead."

"Oh?" says Chas. He looks at me and shrugs.

"You haven't done anything, have you?" The doctor cocks his head, in his helmet, at us.

"Like what?"

"We don't know. We were wondering if you've done something unusual. Something herbal, perhaps? Foreign medicines? Some kind of chemical antitoxin someone gave you? A black market drug? We, um, would need to know of course. For research purposes."

Chas looks at them in disbelief.

I say, "What the fuck are you talking about?"

Chas says, "If we had, wouldn't we tell you? Haven't we told you everything?"

They all begin muttering civilities at once, standing and waiting for the others to get out of the way, not looking at us.

They say, "Excuse us, we didn't mean . . ."

They say, "We didn't mean to be offensive, it's just . . ."

They say, "We'll call soon with the results."

After they leave, I return to my study. There is a filling of the lungs that is supposed to occur in the third week, which I am recreating with strings of transparent yellow crystals.

They don't call that night until nine o'clock. When they do, Chas answers.

They tell him no one, to date, has survived the Visitation. They tell him in no previous case has the Visit been restricted to the brief circuit the Visitor made through our house. They tell him the Visitor should have found us in our beds, gasping for breath, coughing buckets of bile and gore.

When Chas tells me all this, he's laughing. He's his old self. It's as though disreputable babysitters are giving us silly punishments, reprimanding us for our survival.

He challenged them. He asked them about the Visitor. He asked them what it was, who controlled it, why it came, where it came from. He tells me there was absolute silence and then the doctor confessed that they didn't know. They didn't know anything about it, or how it knew when or where to go.

Chas told the doctor, sarcastically, "Maybe when you coat the house in plastic, you provide a tack on the map for it." And there was silence again, a stunned silence, and Chas tells me he got the feeling they hadn't thought of that.

Chas and I sit in silence for a few moments. He says, "I feel great. How do you feel?"

I say, "I could use some air."

"Yes," Chas says, nodding his head at me and grinning. "We could use some air."

The doctor, clearing his throat, told Chas that regardless of the Visit's strange outcome, they had outlined the next procedure for our cases. We would return to the hospital. They would take biopsy samples from our lungs, hearts, and brains. We would undergo a thorough chemo-internal sterilization. They would flush our cavities with saline and chemically treated water. They would drain and replace three-quarters of our blood. They would then be able to give us a prognosis for our survival.

Chas told him we would need a day to set our affairs in order. We put my life-sized chart in the bed and pull the covers up to the queen's chin. We wait until late night for Chas to step out with pruning shears and cut the plastic from the garage doors while I start the car. I go back in for the bag we packed and then decide to leave it. We sit in the car a moment, savoring. We roll down all the windows. The garage door opens and with the headlights off Chas backs out.

The sweet summer air rushes over us. We lean our heads out the windows and open our mouths, stick out our tongues. Chas steers with one hand and holds mine with the other.

Every other house on the street is covered in plastic. We lean back in and look at each other.

"Do you think we're going to die?" I ask.

Chas looks at me and says, "Oh, yeah." He nods his head vehemently. "Definitely. Absolutely. Without a doubt. We're gonna die. We're gonna keel right over." And then we laugh.

We'll die. We will definitely die. At some point, our lungs will fill and then we will empty out, irrevocably. But not now. Now we are stepping beyond the sterility of health. We are going back to being organisms, filthy with germs and dangerous living. Chas might break an arm, get fever blisters. Our lips will chap and our armpits might itch. I may sneeze; I could get the flu. We will experience headaches, neck pains, toe fungus, food poisoning. We might die of cancer or crash the car on the next block, but first we will have this: the wind against our faces, our crazy happiness whipping around the car, the trees sharp against the sky, this night's moment, and these deep breaths of sweet, sweet air.

The Sin Eater

Y ou are looking carefully at the classified ads because living alone means sometimes needing to fill the time. The ad is small, tucked in with other services like lawn mowing and pet sitting. It reads: *Sin Eater 202-417-2055.* Most people would skip right over it, because they don't understand it, or think they don't need it. When you see it though, your hands shake and you circle the notice in black ink.

When you call, you're surprised by the voice that answers. She sounds middle-aged, mean, and hard. She is all business. You try to explain yourself but she interrupts and asks for your address and what time you usually serve dinner. You give her your name, your address, and your phone number as if you know what you're doing.

"I'll be there Thursday at seven." She hangs up before you can ask what she charges, what she eats, what exactly you can expect.

The apartment is an ambush of sentiment. Closets are stuffed with things that you can't stand to see anymore, boxes of pictures and knick-knacks you and your wife bought at flea markets. Half the furniture is missing; half the plants. Your dog, Beanie, is gone, too. Every day you find his hair on your clothes.

All week you have the feeling that there's something to look forward to, but when you try to remember what it is, you realize it's the idea of the Sin Eater you're anticipating. What will she look like? Will she make things better? Does she only help with past sins, or can you get some kind of insurance for the future?

You ask a woman at work if she's heard of Sin Eaters, casually, as if you've only heard about them yourself. Your coworker shakes her head and laughs wistfully. I wish, she says. You're tempted to tell her, but then she would want to hear the whole story, all the details. She would want reasons—and an ending.

Thursday arrives and you're home by five-thirty. You cook. Eggplant parmesan, your mother's recipe, rich with garlic and oil and cheeses. You remember your mother teaching you to cook, telling you what a marvel you'd be to a woman someday. It hurts mid-gut to think of this. You toss a salad. You've bought a bottle of red wine and a loaf of good bread. When the doorbell rings at seven o'clock and you walk to answer it, your mouth is dry with nervousness. You think, actually, that you are going to throw up. Suddenly you feel like everything, your whole life, is riding on this.

You open the door. The Sin Eater is a woman in a tailored, belted, navy blue dress. She might be in her forties or fifties, her skin showing the creases of life. She has thin hair that is pulled into a sharp bun behind her head. Her eyes are dark and her mouth is pinched. She has a small purse over one arm. She leans her head through the doorway and sniffs. She looks at you, frowns, and asks, "You're the one?"

You admit that it is you. Before you can begin the little introduction you've prepared about the meal and what you hope to get from all of this, the Sin Eater pushes past you and into the hallway, sets her purse on the hall table, and says, "No meat? Next time, you'll have to have meat."

You follow her into the kitchen. She stands in the bright light smelling deeply and then she turns to you with raised eyebrows and asks, "How much longer until dinner?"

You tell her it is ready now, but you're not at all convinced that she is what she pretends to be and you're alarmed by the mention of a next time. But before you can say anything she sits at the table where you've set two places and pushes the second mat away with one hand.

"I eat alone," she says. She forces a pursed smile as she breathes in, not a true smile, just the effort of inhaling and smelling that turns her face into a mask.

You put the salad, the breadbasket, and your homemade dressing on the table in front of her. You pour two glasses of wine and take one to her, along with a plate of the eggplant parmesan. She lowers her face into the steam rising from the plate. You feel stupid, standing there in your own kitchen, serving a stranger.

Your stomach is growling. Even though you've never seen one, you think she looks nothing like a Sin Eater. You sip your wine. You look at her, sitting in her prim garb, and you think it's so clever, that ad in the paper luring people like you into this farce. She could be here to make off with the last of your things. She takes her first bite.

Just then she says, "Adulterers always leave out the meat."

You almost drop your glass.

"A sensualist is concerned with garlic, oil, wine. Aromas and aesthetics. You forget the need for sacrifice. It's mostly guilt you want to get rid of, not the sin itself. You don't really regret the sin. The sex was good. There was a real connection." She licks the tines of her fork and continues: "Actually, you may not realize it, but it's the sin of selfishness that you'd like to shake, the sin of self-serving lies and carnal satisfaction. Not the act of infidelity itself. Anyway, it goes deeper than that, of course." Her lips are oily with your salad dressing and the way she eats does not suit anything else about her. Voracious, messy. Even though she uses her fork and knife it seems to you that she is eating with her hands. Her lips and fingers have smeared her wine glass. She uses the edge of her fork to break off a piece of the eggplant, pushing it to the lip of the plate where the red sauce slips over the edge and onto the placemat. When she puts the bite into her mouth, she closes her eyes and growls from the back of her throat. You drink the rest of your wine in a single gulp, and pour another glass.

You remember being with your lover in the parking lot, when she put her hands up to your coat and pulled your mouth down to hers. How the wind and the heat from your touching tongues seemed like a new kind of weather.

The Sin Eater says, "You think if you had made the right choices you wouldn't feel so guilty. You realize you might have made wrong choices, but you can't believe this because it's too late. You never thought you could lie. You feel mean and small."

You are amazed and finally you ask, "You can tell all this from the eggplant?"

She laughs. "No," she says. "It's common to most adulterers." Her laugh reminds you of branches scraping the roof. You want to ask some questions. But it is possible that she is eating your sin. You don't want to distract her.

Suddenly the Sin Eater disappears and your wife is in her chair. Your wife's face is distorted, crying. She looks at you and puts her hands to her cheeks. When she pulls her fingers away the trails of tears come off in thick strings. You press your eyes shut. When you open them the Sin Eater has returned.

You watch her as she continues to find, with her eyes closed, the food on her plate, and lift it to her mouth. She stabs at the eggplant with her fork.

Suddenly you remember your wife's curly hair and slender back the last time she walked away from the building, while you watched from upstairs. How small and defeated she seemed and how you muttered I'm sorry, I'm sorry as you watched her go.

You look up to find that the Sin Eater is staring at you, chewing.

You look into your glass and hear her grunt.

There is a trembling in your chest and you turn and begin to straighten things on the counter.

She says, "Leave that."

"Pardon?" You turn to face her, suddenly annoyed that she is in your house, and when you see her at your table—a small, pinched woman in a blue dress—you think you have really, finally, gone over the edge.

She waves her knife at you and says, "You only organize to distract yourself. How can I do my work if you are distracted? This is why I eat alone. You may sit, if you like, over there." She points at the chair against the wall.

You refill your glass and sit. You look around the kitchen. It is missing things, which your wife has rightfully taken. There is a bare square on the wall where a picture once hung.

"It started a long time ago." The Sin Eater states this, not seeking your agreement. "You've been lying forever. Small lies to make people feel better. Or bigger ones to keep others at bay. You are riddled with lies." She shakes her head and tears a hunk of bread from the loaf. She dips it, carefully, into her wine glass. She holds it up as if to toast you and then pops it into her mouth.

It's not true. You stopped telling lies years ago when you got caught in some stupid one at work. Years ago. And then it was only pretending, not lying. Pretending not to mind that your wife would rather clean or run errands than spend the morning in bed with you. Pretending that you didn't mind the way she opened her mouth at the wrong times when you kissed her. Or that you liked the cheap, tinny earrings she wore with her jeans on Saturdays. No, you didn't begin lying until the time you kissed her goodnight with someone else's neck on your lips.

The Sin Eater's face contorts and she leans over her plate, as if in pain. Her face grows pale and her mouth stretches sideways, like she is going to cry or scream. She breathes in strange, hiccuping gulps. Alarmed, you stand up, but she does not look at you. She only stares, sightlessly, slightly cross-eyed, at the table before her. Finally she leans back in her chair and wipes her sweaty face with a napkin. She sets the linen down on the table and stands, steadying herself with one palm on the table.

You ask, "Are you all right?"

She looks at you and says, "Same time next week. Don't forget the meat."

"But," you begin. "I'm not sure. We haven't talked about your fee. I know nothing about you, or what this is . . . or anything." She walks past you to the hall and picks up her purse. She looks weak, unsteady, her eyes struggling to focus.

"You wouldn't have called," she says, "unless you wanted me to come. Lots of people don't call." She turns and opens the door, and lets herself out.

The next week you grill a flank steak. There are roasted potato wedges, soft inside and crisp outside. There's fresh asparagus and hollandaise, a bottle of Pinot Noir. Grilling the steak, you remember preparing meals with your wife, how she used to sit on the kitchen stool and watch you, read to you, how she loved the way you cooked. She would close her eyes over a pot on the stove and inhale, saying, I would die for your cooking.

When the Sin Eater knocks, you are as nervous as the first time. When you open the door, you have to stop yourself from gasping. She looks terrible. Her eyes are bloodshot and there are purplish bags underneath them. She looks thin and her hair, very straight, has escaped the bun in several places and hangs next to her face in dim strands.

"Oh." You can't think of anything else to say. She waits for you to let her in. You step back and when she passes you can smell her, slightly sour and unwashed.

"Meat," she says, and breathes deeply. She sets her purse on the hall table and walks into the kitchen. She sits in the same seat as before. Her shoulders are hunched. There is a glass of wine already poured for her and she sips from it, wrinkling her nose.

You say, "Look, if this is not a good time for you . . ."

She laughs sharply, that bony laugh. "You can't expect me to look good on a job, now can you?"

You blink at her. She means you. She means your sins.

"Maybe you ought to explain this to me." You put your hands on the counter that stands between you and the table. "How does this work? Am I making you sick? How long do you have to feel bad before we're done?"

She stares at you, her expressionless eyes shiny black buttons. "You should see me after some of my other clients, if you think this is bad." She opens her mouth and belches. She excuses herself indifferently and says, "I'll eat now."

"But," you say. "I don't like being responsible . . ."

She cuts you off with a high snort of laughter.

You are miffed. You set about filling a plate. The meat is cooked just right; the hollandaise is yellow and rich over the asparagus. When you get to the table you realize she has emptied her glass. You frown, retrieve the bottle and refill with wine. You set the bottle on the table. She is after the plate like a starving dog. You can hear her breathing heavily over the food. A piece of meat, too large, slaps her chin as she tries to get it into her mouth. You wish she would stop making your beautiful meal look like slop as she shoves it in.

Suddenly she says, "So many lies," and her voice is distinctly sad. The hair on your arms rises. She drinks, gulping from the glass until it is empty.

As if you are being boiled you can see them frothing, all the lies you've told: to your wife, to your boss, to your friends. You didn't mean to lie about your marriage. You thought, sometimes, I'm probably not in love anymore, but then you would lie. You had to. Your body grew tired of the waiting; it rose of its own accord. Sometimes you would stir when your lover simply looked at you, even before you were lovers. It wasn't you, not your mind or your heart—it was your body that took over, that took care of things. It was time for your marriage to end. Your body knew it.

The Sin Eater lifts the potato wedges, one at a time, with her fork. She places each one in her mouth, eyes closed, and chews.

Standing on a bank high above the river, your lover was wrapped in a blanket that she kept in her car for picnics. The sky was dark with an oncoming storm. You could see two tiny likenesses of yourself reflected in her eyes. You looked like a grown man, a kind man. She folded herself into your arms and you felt how she trusted you. How you felt trustworthy, even though every hour you spent with her was stained with the betrayal of someone else.

The Sin Eater nibbles the skin off the tip of a wedge, working it with her lips like a rodent.

Everything you had was fine. You had a serviceable life. Even as you think it, the word "serviceable" makes you dizzy.

In one of the nightmares, your wife approaches you and touches your cheek with tenderness, brushes your hair back from your forehead. Then she says, "You son of a bitch." Sometimes you dream that a sore on your cheek breaks open and a steady, unstoppable stream of pus pours into the sink.

Waking from these dreams makes you realize how lonely it is to live alone. You miss eating breakfast with your wife, Beanie under the table. You have no right to miss either of them. When you were with your lover, you didn't miss your wife. That was the worst part.

Abruptly, you remember your lover's face, her broad smile, the light of it when she looked at you. You wonder how it will end with her, if it will be her defeated back you see next, and you curl up tight against the hope that it could ever be any different.

The table trembles. You watch the wine slosh in its glass. You look at the Sin Eater and see that she is bright red and shaking from head to toe. As you watch she holds out her hands and flaps them as if they are too hot. More hair comes free from her bun. She looks as if she is going to be sick.

She lets out a huge breath and falls back into her chair, hiccuping.

"Jesus," you say. "Stop. You don't have to eat any more. Just stop." You are afraid she's going to die in your kitchen. You are afraid you are killing her.

She blinks at you and clears her throat. "Is something wrong?" She seems genuinely puzzled.

"Yes!" You get closer to the table, where the remains on her plate look already cold and unappetizing. "It's making you sick. Stop. I'll pay you anyhow."

"I can't stop." She plucks a spear of asparagus and bites off the head. She cocks her head at you and chews. "It's too late. Once I start I can't stop. Besides, it's going very well."

Her face has changed since she came in. Her cheeks are even thinner than before, her eyes alert and narrow. Her fingers are bonier, sharper. She is becoming skeletal.

She lifts her fingertips to the ridge of her brow and says, "If you didn't believe in sin, that would be another story."

"What do you mean?"

"Nothing." She waves the back of her hand at you. "It's just easier for people who don't care, of course."

You ask, "How can you do this to yourself?"

"Do you think I would if I didn't have to?" she snaps. "Believe me. I'd much rather be a grocery bagger." She picks up a sliver of meat and, staring straight at you, slips it into her mouth.

Your wife tried to kiss you one last time, after you'd told her, when you were still trying to fix things. It was slippery and false: a picture of two obscene rubber mouths had flashed in your mind. You winced. She drew back in horror and you both tried to pretend it hadn't happened that way.

The night you told your wife about your lover she stood in the kitchen staring at the ceiling, her fists clenched, begging to wake, as if it was a bad dream. You think about how she was convinced you would love her forever.

You have to sit down. The Sin Eater is watching you. She smiles thinly. One of her lips looks like it's bleeding.

She pushes herself up slowly. Her belt hangs askew on her hips. There is a drop of hollandaise on her dress. Her stockings are torn. She walks out of the kitchen and you see her pause in the doorway, resting against the doorjamb before she goes on.

"Lamb," she says. "Next time, cook lamb."

The week is terrible. You break out so horribly you can't shave. You lose your appetite. The silence in your apartment is brutal and huge, just like when your wife first left. You rush around when you're home, as if everything must be done right away. You drink too much two nights in a row. You put off calling your lover. She doesn't know anything about the Sin Eater. You don't want anyone to know. Violent, repetitive nightmares choke your sleep.

You roast a leg of lamb au jus. You make mashed potatoes, creamed onions, spinach. The lamb is rare and rich with garlic and rosemary. There is blood on the plate when you cut into the meat.

When you answer the door, you are shocked. The Sin Eater looks even worse. Her navy dress hangs from her like an old sheet. It is stained and rumpled. Her hair is completely out of its bun, and the part is crooked. There is a sore on her right eye, a round bulb of redness. Her lips are caked with white and have dried blood in the corners.

"My God."

"Well," she says. "Nobody ever said it was glamorous."

You step back and hold the door. When you reach out to help her by the elbow, she leans slightly into you. You can smell her vividly. She stinks of the unwashed, and a sharp whiff of urine catches you off guard. You resolve that this will be the last meal.

She nods as she enters the kitchen. "Now you've got it. Garlic and lamb. The sensualist learns to accept the sacrifice." She inhales. Beneath her thin crown of hair, her yellow-white skull is visible.

She sits awkwardly in the chair. She rolls the wine glass back and forth by the stem before reluctantly taking a sip. She shudders.

You bring the plate to her. The lamb bones rise sharp and white from the welts of meat. The spinach is deep green. She lifts the meat by the bone and holds it to her mouth, against her lips, as if she is feeling its heat. A dribble of blood runs down her chin. You watch her lick the meat before she carefully takes it in her teeth and bites. She does not bother wiping her chin. She licks and nibbles until the bone is clean. She folds her fingers into a scoop and pushes into the potatoes; she lifts them to her mouth. She pinches wads of spinach and stuffs them into her cheeks.

You imagine your wife asleep. You know that when you look at her, her slight bucktooth will part her lips, making a beautiful blackbird of her mouth. You know that you love her. That you would never hurt her; that it would never occur to you to lie to someone who trusts you so much.

The Sin Eater rubs her fingers on the plate, in the lamb's blood, and smears it over her mouth.

You shake your wife awake. You take her ring finger and break it in half, like a breadstick. You say, I unmarry you.

The Sin Eater fills her hands with potatoes and begins licking them. Her tongue is whitish and bumpy. It makes a rasping sound on her palms.

You start to say, "Look," and the Sin Eater glances up but doesn't stop eating. Suddenly you feel faint, feverish, ill. She lowers her head to the table and licks the plate.

Your wife begs you to change your mind. She makes promises, her voice cracking. She asks you to give up your lover. You realize that you know something she doesn't. It isn't about your body, like you thought. It isn't about the adultery. It is you and her. You envision a picture of yourselves as if you were a different species. You are not alike. You are not at all alike.

You bend at the waist, your upper body suddenly too heavy, and you stare at the floor a minute, your nose running, the blood rushing to your head. It is not about her, now. It is about you, what you want and must pursue.

The Sin Eater has fallen still. Her head hangs to her chest. She is snoring lightly.

You shake her awake. She is bleary, drunk with food; she can't keep her eyes open. She blinks, licks her lips with her swollen tongue. She looks at you and nods. She leans closer and you can see the dry skin around her nostrils, the hard yellow rocks in the corners of her eyes. Her pupils contract and grow large and black. There is a pulling inside you, not quite sexual, but deeper, as if a hand is digging within your body, feeling for something, or maybe drawing something out, a giant white root, a tendon, a bone. You sit there, as still as you can, and wait for her to finish.

Frances, Upstairs

F rances' moods ruled over us. Frances, drunk. Frances, mad.
Frances, singing. Frances, in love. Frances, crying. Frances,
drunk. Frances, mad.

My mother and I rented the first-floor apartment in a sagging
green house, and Frances rented the one above ours. The house was
bad enough, with cracked windows and drafty wooden floors, but
worse was the thinness of the walls, which allowed us to hear
Frances all the time. Her arguments, her dog, her lovers. We often
heard her say, *I can't take it anymore*, but we were witnesses to all
she could and did take.

My mother huffed and muttered, sent some notes on cards
patterned with daisies asking our landlord to do something about
Frances, but he never replied.

We spoke of Frances every day. We listened through the walls and my mother's bedroom windows, which looked out onto Frances' front porch. Almost every day, her ratty Chihuahua got away from her, and Frances would swoop and lurch around the yard in her tight jeans or leather pants, reaching under the rhododendrons, crooning for her *Little Tiny*. Often, I would see Little Tiny's ruched three-inch back depositing milky turds on our part of the lawn, brown clumps that would stay forever because we didn't bother to go outside.

My mother hated that dog. "Little Tiny what?" She would say. One good day, she even made a joke of it: "Rotten Ill-Behaved, she should have called him. Stupid Ignorant." But my mother's jokes were rare and they didn't tend to make her laugh twice.

When Frances caused a stir, my mother often asked me, "What is it now?" as if I knew. Just because I didn't mind peering through the blinds, or pressing my ear to the flimsy wall, didn't mean I should know why Frances was upset, although I did. I got very good at piecing together Frances' moods. It wasn't much different than living with parents, really. If you were listening, you knew what was coming. For example, I knew my father was having an affair at least two months before he left us. Any idiot could tell.

I was fourteen that miserable winter after my parents divorced and my mother, in a fit of stupid independence, moved us to a new town.

"A fresh start," she'd said, though there was nothing fresh about the run-down neighborhood we'd had to move into, or the neighbors themselves, who limped and had gray teeth and stood on the curb staring at nothing.

I learned how to curse from Frances. In our old neighborhood of houses and driveways and lawns, I didn't know anybody who cursed, but Frances cursed enough to paper a wall. It wasn't the variety of the words, but the way she used them that captivated me. Repetitions, pacing, pairings. She screamed curses into the phone, out the window, off the front porch. *Shit* ten times, going up and down a scale, before you heard her heavy footsteps thumping out the door and slam! *Fucking fuck!* Then a glass breaking, or a thump. *Fuckingbitchwhorefuck!* The slam of a phone on its cradle.

My mother was nothing like Frances. My mother was pale and thin and quiet. The kind of woman who scoured the kitchen twice a week and vacuumed daily. She wore light-colored blouses and plain skirts. She wore flat shoes that made no noise when she walked. We watched certain television programs on certain nights and then we turned off the set and read books. My mother read popular mysteries and romances. I did my homework at the kitchen table. We ate dinner at seven. After, we had small bowls of ice cream. Often, during ice cream, we heard Little Tiny chasing balls wildly in the kitchen overhead. When the ball hit a wall with a thump and Little Tiny's claws scratched desperately at the floor only to be followed by a second thump and a high animal shriek, my mother reliably shook her head and said something about ruining the floors.

Frances had a lot of boyfriends. All of them made her drink and curse, but I never thought this was entirely their fault. Juan and Victor were the main ones, though there were others who didn't last long before Juan came and scared them away. I hated Juan, because he beat Frances and was a runty, mean-faced man. When he beat her, our walls shook and her moans and yelps seeped into our rooms.

I called the police a couple of times. When they came, nothing happened. They knocked on the door and Frances sent them away. So I quit calling.

Once, someone else called an ambulance. Someone who was up there begging Frances to stop, to calm down, to breathe, to be reasonable. Frances sounded in bad shape that night, heaving panting breaths, wheezing loudly, as if she was being choked, occasionally gasping *I can't take it anymore.* When the ambulance came and lit up my mother's bedroom with flashes of red, I went to watch through a finger's width of raised blind. I heard them carrying Frances down, her awful voice cursing them the whole way, and I saw them wheel her to the ambulance, her huge mass of curly hair like an animal atop her head. She was sitting up on the rolling bed, giving one of them the finger, and she didn't look small, or sick, or anything. She looked like someone who had no reason to make such a fuss. She looked like someone who was breathing just fine.

My mother worked in a new office that didn't seem all that different from her old office. Her work bored me. In fact, I think the only thing interesting about my mother, aside from the fact that she was my mother and I loved her, was that her husband left her for a stranger from a temp agency, making a big splashy divorce of it. But we didn't talk about any of that after awhile.

My father called me to see if I needed anything. I didn't know what I needed, so our conversations were short.

I hadn't made friends at school. It was a very different school, and the work was too easy for me. This didn't endear me to my classmates, who couldn't have cared less about the development of Western civilization and were not impressed by my knowledge of the Roman emperors. Caesar was a cheesy salad dressing, one girl noted, and anyone who didn't like it could kiss her ass.

On Fridays, we ordered a pizza from the shop down the street. Mom brought home a movie with big-name stars. We ate cheese pizza, drank Coke with ice, and watched the movie. It would be a nice evening, for a little while. Frances didn't usually get started until later, around 11:00. We'd have switched to the news by then.

FUCK YOU. Fuck you, too. Fuck off. Asshole. Don't you call ME a bitch. Why you even call me up, you hate me so bad? I sure as hell didn't call your sorry ass. Don't even. FUCK YOU. Fucking. Fuck. Fuck You. Then Frances would launch into a stream of curses as she stomped around her rooms doing who knows what. Phone calls were better than the in-person arguments. Phone calls usually ended sooner.

Whenever Frances started, Mom started. She would fuss around, worrying the floors with her broom. She straightened tables and knick-knacks. Washed the butter dish. Refolded the towels already folded on the bathroom's single shelf until there was nothing else to do, and she had to go to bed.

Occasionally, if Juan were there, they'd have friends over. Big round laughs would boom down. Fat laughs. *That ain't right. Hahaha.* But they got smaller and meaner as the night went on, and we knew when we heard the footsteps on the stairs that the fights would begin. Juan was jealous and petty and it sounded like, since he'd gotten out of prison, he heard nothing but rumors of what Frances had done while he was away. He liked to go over these rumors late, after drinking. *You been with Ramon. I know you been with Ramon, so don't lie to me. Slut.* Sometimes, he sweet-talked: *Ain't I your man? Baby, ain't I your man?* But it always turned hard with a terrible thump and a shout: *Then why the fuck can't you be true, bitch?*

In school, I didn't really have to concentrate, so I stopped trying. I would spend a whole class looking at the French teacher's squat legs. A math teacher's chalky fingers. I could watch a moustache, a facial tic, a pair of earrings for a solid fifty-five minutes. Nobody knew me, anyhow. And they wouldn't know me, because I could tell I was already changing.

While it seemed I would never find a friend, much less a boyfriend, Frances had so many. I didn't understand. One guy, Victor, just walked the dogs and paid the bills. Sometimes he picked Frances up in the morning, always for something ordinary like breakfast at the diner, or a ride to the doctor's. When he dropped her off, after he'd taken Little Tiny outside, she would walk him to the car and give him a kiss. Only one kiss each time. I couldn't believe that. Some of the other guys couldn't even get in the door for all her kissing. One morning, though, Victor came too early. Frances was still drunk from the night before and she threw him out. In the cold, white light she pounded her fist over her breast and shouted at him, *I never felt nothing for you! Nothing!* It made me gasp, it was so mean, and his face was so pale, but not long after, he showed up again and walked Little Tiny, and sometimes he came to her mailbox and took the gas and phone bills away with him.

There was another guy, a no-name guy, who brought his guitar. They sang songs all night until Frances got pitiful. Then they would have sex and she'd cry all the way through, sometimes interrupting herself to say, *No, here, over here. That's the spot, baby,* but then she'd go back to crying and we'd hear his footsteps leaving after awhile. I worried about my mother. Did it make her lonely? It made me tingle, sometimes, wondering what they were doing, but then Frances' sloppy voice drifted into my room again and I wasn't curious anymore.

Sometimes during Frances' fights, I would get up from my fold-out couch in the living room and walk into the dark bedroom where my mother lay staring at the ceiling. She slept in long flannel nightgowns with high necks because she hated a draft. All I might say would be, "Do you hear it?" And she would nod. Or sometimes I would say, "Should we call somebody?" But she'd only stare at me questioningly until I went back to bed.

Under my blankets, I would listen to Frances' voice rising and falling, catching horribly with sobs and self-pity, and I could feel how under it I became so small. How I shrank in my bed until I could imagine myself from elsewhere in the room, just a heap, like the dead spider on the sill.

For my mother's birthday, I planned an evening. We went out for Chinese and ate ourselves silly on eggrolls and Hunan shrimp. We'd both put on nice blouses to make it special, and my mother even wore pink lipstick. There was a fish tank in the lobby of the restaurant, and we stood for a long time on our way out, pointing out fish and coral and crabs, soothed by the slow bubbling pull of the water. I felt I could have stood there forever, calm and full, with my mother beside me.

We got home and I set up the Boggle game on the coffee table. I put Mom's favorite, Karen Carpenter, on the stereo. We got out the score pads and were in the middle of the second game when Frances started.

Cocksuckingbastardmotherassholefucking GET. OUT. OF. MY.

HOUSE.

My mother's face crumpled. She sank into her bones. Her eyes hollowed, as though she hadn't eaten in months.

Don't tell me what to do, you stupid bitch. It was Juan, sounding mild in comparison to Frances.

You think you got some fucking RIGHT to me or something? Some kind of SPELL on my pussy? Is that it? Take your big-fucking-ass, and get out of my house. Right now. You deaf? YOU DEAF? Little Tiny scrambled off a couch or chair with a tiny thump, and then he pitched into hysterical barking. *Yap-yap-yp-yap-yap!*

Juan was roused, but his words slurred: *Here I pay for all this sweet stuff and you gonna be like this?*

You think you the only one who buys me things? No. No. You aren't even the second in line. You're last. Dumbfuckingdrugaddictmotherfuckingsoapfucker.

Yap-yap-yp-yap-yap, went Little Tiny.

NO! A glass broke against the wall.

That's it, bitch.

You mean NOTHING to me! FUCK-ING NO-THING!

Someone shoved someone, because my mother's Dutch plates rattled against the wall. My fists were clenched so hard I could feel my nails cutting into the palms of my hands. I felt guilty for trying to make my mother happy, when we both knew this would happen. It was awful to be in our house and out of our house and in our skins and there was nowhere, nowhere at all for either of us to go. What kind of fool was my mother? Why had she brought me here? Why was she such a stupid, ignorant dumbass? There was no one to ask.

Yapyapyapyapfuckyouyapyapyapfuckyoumotherfuckerthisisn'tyo urstohavenomoregetitfromoneofyourcrackheadwhoresyapyapyapyap yaplyeeeeeeee!

My mother stared blindly at the floor. I gritted my teeth, hating her and hating my father and Little Tiny and pathetic Victor and the guitar player and Juan and most all, Frances, who couldn't let us have a single second's peace, not one single night she didn't have to steal, everyone's attention on Frances, poor Frances, mad Frances, crying Frances, all for Frances, always, always, always.

I got up and went to the kitchen and grabbed as many juice glasses as I could hold. I scrambled to our door, wrested it open, and ran outside. It was cold and dark and there was Little Tiny shit everywhere, but I didn't care; I ran as fast as I could to the front of the house and I was the one screaming then, smashing glasses against her door, and screaming, "*SHUT-THE-FUCK-UP! SH—UT THE MO—THER—FUCK—ING FUCK UP! I CAN'T TAKE IT ANYMORE!*"

Glass was flying in the porch light and some part of me was bleeding, and the door opened. Dumbass Frances stood there, her thick hair bunched, lopsided and wild, in a rubber band on the side of her head, mascara streaking her face, her lipstick smeared, and next to her, pinched-face Juan. I could see that chickenshit was holding a gun and I didn't care. I leaned in the doorway to where I could smell whatever fried food she'd made and I stared into her thick, unfocused eyes, and whispered, "Nobody cares about you, Frances. Not one goddamn person."

She blinked at me, and there was a long pause while we stared into the silence after their screaming and my screaming and all the glass-breaking.

Then Frances turned to Juan and said, "Who the fuck *is* this kid?"

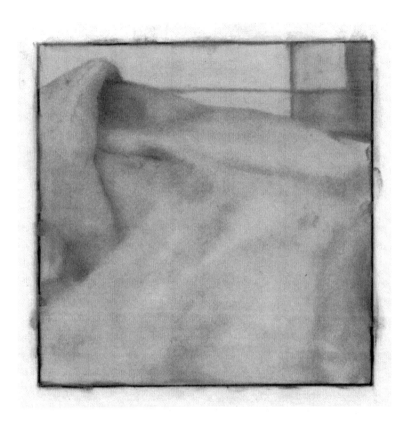

I See Her

I stand at the hotel window looking through the glass cleaner I have sprayed and forgotten to wipe away. Three stories below, on the path in the dunes, a woman was murdered. There is nothing left to indicate what happened, but I can see her all the same.

She is standing naked, halfway up the dune, her hair whipping across her face as if she's already being scratched off a page. Her breasts and the dark thatch of hair between her legs are startling on her bright-skinned body. She is a tall woman.

The smell of cleaner stings my eyes, so I raise my cloth and wipe the pane in circles, finishing with neat horizontal rows.

I cannot go into her room, though it has shown up on my list today. The policemen are through with it now and someone has to vacuum and dust all that black powder they've left. It's on my list because I'm the most thorough housekeeper here, but I can't go in. I can't even put my hand on the doorknob. Her things will be gone, I know, but I am afraid there will still be something, a used washcloth, a lingering perfume.

We have all been questioned and questioned again. My eyes fill when I shake my head no and say I didn't know her. It's true, I never did speak with her, or glimpse her more than a couple of times, but wasn't I the one who gave her the towels that she used to dry her body the last time she washed? Wasn't I the one who made her bed, who thumped the pillows full, who pulled the clean sheets up and tucked them tight so that when she slid into them she would feel safe and warm? I do the same for everyone but something about her made me extra careful, as if she deserved my best. I think of her sleeping, the cotton cool against her skin after a day at the beach and a big seafood dinner; I can see her hair on the pillow, her smooth white neck half turned in sleep.

They cannot find the knife or the dress she was wearing, but what do you expect? They are small-time beach town cops and the most they've ever done is catch a houseful of adults sniffing cocaine through fifty-dollar bills. This is their chance to be like the cops on television, and they ask questions you know they've only ever heard on some show, just like you, but they lean back in their chairs, their gun belts squeaking, and you know that when they go home they will tell their wives about the case and a whole new feeling will enter them, a feeling of importance and virility and purpose. They'll never catch the one who did it. I have a feeling he's all the way up the coast by now, receiving the news about his girlfriend with shock and alarm and grief. Don't ask me how I know. Sometimes these feelings come on so strong they can't be anything but truth.

I see her body on the dunes as the sun is rising over the grasses, and she is dark with blood. I'm not so upset by the vision: she is no more dead or alive than the hundreds of carcasses you find on a beach every day, empty crabs and dead jellies, the tiny spines of half-eaten fish. I think there are probably worse places to be dead.

When I go home at night and peel potatoes or mix egg into the hamburger for Gene's meatloaf, I wonder if she ever made meatloaf for a man she no longer loved, but I think probably not—when she got tired of something, she just got up and moved on.

When I was a kid and we lived in the trailers down near the cove, there was a girl there named Jolene. She was like that, too. She never waited for someone else to get in the water first, or climb the pier legs, or steal the first six-pack. She was always first and she didn't waste her time like those of us too afraid. She just went right on swimming, or climbing, or drinking, a universe unto herself.

One day there was a dress lying across the woman's bed, silk and red and bold and even then, before I knew what would happen to her, that's what I thought: this is the dress of a woman who does not wait for things to change.

Every night Gene asks when dinner will be done, but ever since the murder he hangs around the kitchen wanting to know if the police have any leads. Leads, he says, like this is one of his usual words.

What I want to say, but do not, is that it's not so clear to me that this man is just a plain murderer. When I see him, he's very neat and tidy, a white ironed shirt tucked into his pants, which is more than I can say for Gene, with a good leather belt through all of his belt loops. His hair is sprayed and lifts in a flap when the wind catches it. He's not severe or all that alarming, even when his face grows angry. She is far more dangerous-looking, her feet spread for balance on the dune, her mouth open like a red sore streaming curses, her hair snatching around her face, her naked body bright as a knife against the dark.

She's the one screaming at him, and he looks almost frightened, whether it's because he already knows what he's going to do or not I can't say, but there's something at work that isn't your usual balance of who did what. Regardless, I answer Gene the same every night, Nope, no leads.

This gives Gene the opportunity to deliver his two cent speech about wasted tax dollars and wild goose chases, after which he goes back to his television while I return to mixing the bread crumbs and ketchup into the meat. Sometimes I can't believe how stupid Gene is, how for a man who can do so many things with his hands he's just a zombie repeating everything he's ever heard. As if his only purpose in life is to fill in conversation's empty blanks with the usual replies.

When I get to work the next morning, the back of the hotel is teeming with police. I can see Len and Sammy and William hauling out all the old crap from under the Tiki bar that reaches out to the dunes. They've already been under there once but I suppose they've run out of other ideas, so now they're tearing the place apart. I'm interested to see what was beneath a storage area completely exposed to the elements. Whose idea was that I wonder, leaving only latticework and darkness to protect things from the ocean? All day I look down from the rooms I'm cleaning to watch them pull some beautiful, weather-beaten things out and onto the sand.

At lunch I wander out, most of the guys now gone, just old furniture scattered halfway up the dune. As I walk, I feel the sand behind me and I'm thinking just over there is where she died, and I look back at the furniture and then I know: these old things must have heard her die. I become attached to them, then. This table, this chair, the old rotting picnic bench and lifeguard stand. They've heard what I can see. I stand still and listen for a moment.

When Len comes out I ask him if I can have this table here, and he heaves a sigh that's intended to mean you're such a stupid woman, and then he says, For God's sake, this isn't a yard sale, and I get mad because they all talk to me like this; just because I'm quiet they think I'm stupid, and I say, What are you going to do, put it all back under there? And I can see he hasn't thought about that yet and he looks at me funny, like he wishes I would disappear, and then he says, Just take the damn table.

So I do.

I take it home and after I've made pork chops and macaroni and cleaned it all up I go out to the garage and look over the table. It's mildewed. I get out some sandpaper and begin to sand it and after awhile it gives it up and I hear the small, sad groan. Not a sharp bark of fear or a piercing scream, but this little groan—half air escaping and half wistful goodbye. It's so faint, such a weak noise to leave the world with that it all comes on me in a rush and I lean over the table, put my arms right down in the sawdust I've made, and weep for her, for her foolishness and bravado. Whatever the argument was it's over now and would have been even if she weren't dead. That's how arguments go. She must have known he had a temper.

After a while Gene comes out, stands in the doorway of the garage, embarrassed that I'm on my knees with my head on a half-sanded table, and says nervously, Everything okay out here, and I don't answer him, I just don't have any words for him, used or new, and after a moment he turns back and shuts the door after him.

I can't even begin to tell him anything about myself. I don't know that he'd ever understand. It's as if all these years I've been silent I've traveled so far that I don't even speak his language anymore.

Someone else cleaned her room. I feel sad that I couldn't do it but the fact is I'm needing to get her off my mind and I can't. I remember one time when I saw her, walking through the lobby to the bar, and she smiled over her shoulder at the person behind her who held the door and that smile, the genuine friendliness, the smile of a person without fear, it's just stuck in me like a bone. The whole living-dead thing, how she lit up the beach that night and then went dark for always, it digs at me.

I can't sleep either, with Gene in the bed beside me, farting and snoring, all his breaths clouding the room. I can't stand it.

Finally, one night I get up and put on some clothes and I leave the house. I've never done this before, at least not since I was a girl and went out with my cousin smoking cigarettes. It's a blue night, with a half-moon lighting the way and the pines stirring in the breeze. I can't believe I don't do this more often. I feel more at peace than I can ever remember.

It's a half-mile to the hotel through empty streets and I walk slow, taking my time, listening to the ocean's murmur as I get closer.

We all die alone I know but somehow that's not the point. It's not the dying that matters but what you've been, and what I always think about when I think about my own death is that there will be no one who says, this was the heart of her. They will go to the funeral service and say prayers they don't mean or even want to understand, they'll tell Gene I was a good woman and he'll say, yes, she was, and they'll have no idea how many nights I wished he would just quit breathing so I could get up and leave; they won't know anything about me except I was a good wife, that meatloaf maker, that maid from the Seascape Hotel. I feel like I understand something about this woman who has just died, and I want to give her better than I'll get.

I walk across the parking lot of the hotel and when I reach the sand I take off my shoes and let my feet sink into the coolness. It feels terrific and when I think this I laugh—a word like "terrific" doesn't come up for me so often, but this is what the sand between my toes feels like. I walk up the dune, excited to see the ocean, this ocean that I've seen every day of my life and in every weather; I'm excited to see it, and when I come over the top of the dune, there it is, a glossy dark sea, so dark it looks like another sky.

I walk about halfway down the dune, to where I know she last lay, and I put my body down where I'm sure hers was. I spread my arms wide and wiggle my backside deeper, so the sand curves to the shape of me. I close my eyes and listen to the ocean rocking itself onto the waiting shore.

She's all sandy when she comes up over the dunes. I see her shouting at him, plunging each leg into the sand as she descends. She is naked, as beautiful probably as she's ever been, but neither of them knows this because they are too concerned with hurting each other with words. He has refused her something, this is the problem, and I wish I could rise and talk some sense into her, but she's wild standing there, her hair across her face, her eyes shining dark. He stands, hesitating on the crest above her, and I'm curious because he looks so little like a murderer that I can't imagine he's really going to do it, so I look closer, peer into his face, and there in the corner of his eye I see the hardness of something that he will never forgive, or maybe she's denied him her heart. I see suddenly how he wants her whole self, almost more than just love or sex, he wants to own her and this frightens me, startles me; it is the same feeling that I have about her: something I want to own, or maybe something I want to be, and then I think that if this is it, he has to kill her, because he and I will never measure up.

I look back at her and she stands screaming at him, her mouth moving in an awful, ugly way and I see that she belongs entirely to herself, that she's not afraid of him, or of anyone seeing her; she is at the end of her life, the last minute of her life, and there's something about her, her nakedness, her legs spread slightly, her fists clenched, that suggests she's ready for it, that she's waiting for it.

The knife flashes out as if it's part of him. He steps forward and with one sweeping motion, like a violinist drawing his bow, he slashes it across her neck and she opens wide, falls back in the sand, a small groan, half sigh, half wistful goodbye, escaping her.

She is on a slant, like I am now, and the blood pumping from her heart spills out of her neck in wet spreads, like the tide.

I lie like that all through the night. I'm cold. It's just September, but in a couple of weeks it will be too cool to do this. The first gray light breaks over me, just a glimmering of morning, and I can see her there, beautiful in her blood. When I open my eyes she has risen. She is walking toward the water, but this time she knows I am coming, too, and she turns and waits for me.

The Boy

I' m dumping drawers of utensils into boxes. I enjoy the dangerous way they clatter, the way the pronged fork sticks out, the thermometer's bared needle. So much crap. Spatulas, basters, pie servers. I wonder whose stuff this is, who I was that needed such things. For a year now I have lived on convenience foods, five-minute showers, plastic bags for traveling. I have lived in one corner of this house, like a spider, a water bug.

I stop and stare at a takeout menu from a restaurant that's been out of business for years. I haven't brushed my teeth in days, or combed my hair. I've been wearing the same jeans for a week, so soft they feel damp and flap at my ankles. Moving is a no man's land. You are neither here nor there, and everyone has forgotten you because they believe you are too busy to be concerned with living.

There's a dog barking outside. It's been barking for a few

minutes. I kick aside the box I've been packing and walk to the front door.

In the street, beyond the azalea bushes, the dog is acting crazy, leaping and barking at something out of sight.

"Hey dog, what's going on?"

That's when I see the little boy, about six or seven years old. He's standing and holding a backpack with one hand. The dog snarls and leaps, but bounces back as though he's been stopped by an invisible shield.

"Don't move," I yell, and run back inside, thinking I'll need a jacket or something in case the dog attacks me. Inside, though, I realize my jacket is packed.

I run back outside, calling, "Here I am, here I am," but the boy is gone. The dog is gone. In the bushes there is a horrific stench, as if something big, bigger than a squirrel or a chipmunk, has died. I look. There is nothing. There's no sign of the boy or the dog.

I've packed the lamps, so I work by the few overheads, one in the kitchen, one in the dining room. They're so bright they make everything seem shallow, including my own shadow, thin and sharp beside me. As I finish packing each room, I push everything against the wall, furniture, stacks of boxes, rolled rugs. It looks like I'm having a dance. As if I'm planning a party where it will be standing room only.

I sleep on a mattress on the living room floor and look at the brown boxes filled with my things. I'm tempted to just throw them all away while I can't see what's inside.

Barking wakes me. The same hysterical bark. I crawl to the window and look out. The dog is standing at the break in the azalea bushes, barking its head off. The boy, with his backpack, is sitting on the lawn.

"Hey," I call out softly, in case I'm imagining him. He turns his head and looks up at the window. A delicate face, a bowl shape of dark hair.

"Hey," he says back.

"Stay there." I stand slowly, keeping my eye on him as long as I can. I throw the front door open and peer through the screen. The dog, startled, stops barking. The boy waits for me.

I step out on the front porch. The dog resumes its barking, short, sharp yelps. I walk down the creaky porch steps and the boy stands up. There's a warm breeze.

The stench hits me. It's so overpowering, thick, and alive that I almost fall; it smells like rotting fish, like heat, shit, death. I gasp and put my hands over my nose. The boy watches me.

"The dog is following me," he says sadly, "because I stink."

I step onto the grass and my vision shifts inward, the house, the sky, the bushes, the night stars disappear as the tunnel grows black and wide. My legs go soft. I am falling.

When I awake, it's cold. The bluish light of dawn is over the neighborhood. I am soaked with dew. I'm freezing. My face has been in the grass. I sit up. The boy and the dog are gone.

Inside, I have to rummage through several boxes to find a sweater. I strip off my clothes and pull it on. I wrap myself in the sheet and blanket and sit on the mattress. I can't stop shivering.

Hallucinating and passing out in the grass seem to be clear examples of ways in which I am inappropriate about life. I count twenty other reasons why I am a failure. I count four reasons why it is stupid to sell the house. I wish for simple worries: weight, getting toilet paper in the house, what to cook for dinner. I think about people who read flyers during the holidays, looking for perfect gifts. I think about people who drive two extra miles for cheaper aspirin. I wish I were like them.

I lie down and stare at the room. There are knots of dust and hair on the floor. The sight of them, all that's left of my history in the house, makes me shudder.

I'm out back, in the small garage, cleaning the years of accumulated junk into garbage bags. Coffee cans full of odd screws and nails and unidentifiable bits of metal. Old clothes, a bicycle with rotten tires. All the photo albums are out here. I discover them and toss them in a bag. After a few minutes, I pull them back out and flip through them.

I look so ruddy. And innocent. We're on bicycles. Or swimming. My hair long for a few years, or short. A party in the backyard, which looks great in the pictures but is now tall with weeds and sticks that have fallen from the oak trees during storms. I'm smiling in the pictures. It's a hollow feeling, to see myself smiling and know I wasn't happy. I wish I could be fooled.

I smell him first and then the dog whines. The dog is in the doorway of the garage. He wags his tail. He's a mangy dog, a brown mutt with orange splotches. The boy is behind me, sitting on an old sawhorse that once belonged to my father-in-law.

The boy says, "Don't faint, please."

I press my tongue to the roof of my mouth to block out the smell.

"Who are you?" I ask nasally.

"I'm afraid of that dog," he says. "He's following me because of this smell and I don't know what to do."

"What *is* that smell?" I peer at him. He looks fairly clean; there's no obvious reason he should smell.

"I don't know," the boy says. He looks at the dog and swings his legs. After a moment he stops swinging them, looks back at me, and says intently, "but I'm *afraid*."

"Maybe there's something in your backpack that smells?"

He climbs down and brings the pack over to me.

"It's just my schoolwork," he says. "Here's my math homework, here's my spelling. I drew this picture during art hour and this is my special tiger eraser." The paper is the same children have always used, with its large dotted lines. The math is subtraction. The boy is not good at this. The spelling words are done carefully and correctly: door, queen, walk, think, coat, apple. The drawing is outlined in pencil, colored in with crayon. There is a house, two blue trees, some bushes. A green dog.

"Whose house is this?"

"My house."

"Is that your dog?" I point to the dog at the door. He's not barking, I notice. He wags his tail, once, when we look at him.

"No, not him. That's my dog, there." He points to the picture.

"Oh. I see. Is he really green?"

He looks at me and giggles. "No." He giggles again.

"Why are you laughing?"

"Your voice sounds funny."

"It's 'cause I'm holding my nose, mister." I look at him. His eyes are a bright brown under his bangs. A rosy mouth, pointy chin. He's amazingly sweet. Somebody must be looking for him, I think. If he's real. "So, tell me." I walk over and put the photo albums back into the garbage bag. "Why don't you go home?"

"I can't."

"Why not?"

"Can't you smell me?" I've upset him. He shakes the paper with the house drawing at the dog. "I stink! I stink! This dog won't let me!"

"Have you tried to wash?"

"I want to wash," says the boy, his eyes filling with tears, "but I can't go hooooooome." He lets the paper drift to the floor, drops the bag, and stands crying. The dog barks.

I let my tongue off the roof of my mouth for a second and there it is: a bloating smell, vomit and blood and rotting fur. I clamp my nose shut with two fingers, my stomach heaving.

The dog's barking bounces off the walls of the garage.

I say, "What if I let you wash in my tub?" The boy is hunched over, his face wet with tears. He looks up at me and blinks.

"What about the dog?" he asks.

"What about it?"

"Can he come?"

Everywhere he touches, he leaves yellow stains. From his fingertips, a dust, like pollen. Small finger lines on the back of my hand, on the door where he's held it open for the dog.

We walk through the half-empty house. The dog follows us. I lift the boy and carry him up the stairs. He is slightly clammy from crying. I can feel his small palm on my back. The dog's nails click on the floors behind us.

In the bathroom, I turn on the faucet. The old shower curtain has already been torn off and thrown away. There is shampoo and a bar of soap. The boy and the dog stand watching the steam rise.

I notice the afternoon sun flickering in the window, blocking out maple shadows on the wall. Afternoon sun, my favorite. I feel good for the first time in months.

I ask the boy, "Do you need help getting undressed?"

"No," he says. He sets his backpack down on the black-and-white tile floor. He takes off his sneakers, his pants, his shirt. He stands in his small white underwear and white socks.

"Are you shy? Do you want me to leave?"

"No!" he says. His eyes are wide. "That water looks so hot! Will it burn me?"

I laugh. "It's not so hot; besides, it has to be warm enough to get that smell off, right?"

"Right." He removes his socks, slowly, peeling them off and dropping them in balls on the floor. He stares again at the water. "What if I slip and fall when I'm getting in?"

"I'll help you."

He takes off his underwear and waits in the middle of the bathroom, uncertain. He's so small I can't believe he's human. Twig arms, tiny dot nipples. His skin is so thin and pale I can almost see through to the slender bones, the bean of his heart.

He holds out his hands, smiling vaguely. I pick him up, his arms so fragile I feel as if I could pop them off, and lower him, two small feet first, into the tub.

He shrieks lightly, blinking at his feet.

The Boy

After a minute, he sits down. Yellow, bright as Easter egg dye, floods into the water. The dog barks. I assume the smell is worse when the boy is wet.

He squeals with delight: "It's warm!"

I lather up the bar of soap and begin on his back, the twin scapulas like miniature fins. He splashes his hands, dark yellow streaks spilling from his fingertips. I scrub with my hands: his back, his arms, his neck, his chest, his feet. I get his hair damp, scooping water up the back of his neck. He giggles and hunches his shoulders. My palms turn a deep yellow. I dab shampoo on his scalp and scrub with my nails.

"Ouch," he says mildly. He makes up a song, a string of sounds that pleases him.

I rinse his hair with an old plastic cup from under the sink, pouring water over his head and pushing it away from his face with my hands. He sings. He looks like a wet little animal with his hair slicked back, his pointed pink scalp. I feel a huge affection for him.

"Stay here," I say. "I've got to find some towels."

He adds "okay" to his string of song sounds. The dog watches, unmoving as I step over him.

I open the laundry closet, pleased to find I haven't yet packed the towels. With a start, I realize I'm not holding my tongue to the roof of my mouth anymore. I'm breathing normally. I laugh.

I'm walking back across the hall when I realize his singing has stopped.

In the bathroom, the tub is full of clean, clear water. I set the towels down on the toilet seat. I reach out and touch the soap, which is dry.

I'm sitting on a kitchen chair, crying and talking to myself. The tears that stream from my eyes feel good and hot on my cheeks. I let my words run together into a wail. I'm so upset. I say this aloud and it soothes me. "I'm so upset! I'm so upset!" I pinch the fabric of my jeans. Sometimes I moan with my mouth open, which sounds bottomlessly sad, and satisfies me.

Eventually, I stop. I wipe my eyes with paper napkins from the chicken place where I got my dinner a few nights ago. On the napkins, there are garish, bulbous red letters. I stare blankly at the design and then blow my nose on a napkin. I toss another at the garbage and miss.

"You have bad aim," he says.

I turn around. He's standing in the kitchen doorway. His hair is wet and combed to one side. He's wearing one of my T-shirts, which reaches to his knees. The dog moves past him and lies down under the table. I can't smell anything but shampoo.

"You're supposed to be in the tub!"

He shrugs. "I'm hungry," he says.

All I've left out is peanut butter and bread. I take the jar of peanut butter, the half loaf of bread, and a knife over to the table. He pulls out the other chair and sits down, just his head showing above the tabletop. I spread a slice for him.

"Not too much, please," he says. He's looking at me strangely. Glancing and then looking away. I realize he is trying to be polite and not stare.

"What?" I ask him.

"Nothing." he says. He accepts the peanut butter bread and sniffs. "I like this peanut butter. I don't like the crunchy kind that pokes you in the mouth."

"Nope, me neither."

He looks up at me as he chews. I smile at him. He finishes his bite and swallows. He looks at me again and says, "Were you crying?"

I put my hand to my face. I'm sure it's all blotchy and red and pitiful-looking. I nod my head yes.

"Why were you crying?"

"I feel like I'm going crazy."

"*You?*" He's so shocked by this he points a finger at me to be sure he understands what I mean.

I can't help but laugh, he makes me feel so much better. He laughs, too, his mouth open. He has peanut butter bread smashed inside his cheeks. It makes me laugh harder. I spin a finger next to my head to show how crazy I am. We laugh more. He chews and kicks his foot rhythmically under the table.

"If you're crazy," he announces, "then I'm crazy, too." He reaches for the jar, begins spreading another slice. He gets peanut butter on his thumb and licks it off. I look over at him, his face shiny and scrubbed. The dog snuffles under the table, rolls onto its side, stretches its legs out, and sighs.

"You're a good person," I say.

His mouth is full, but he says, "Me, too."

"I said *you* were a good person."

"I thought you meant you," he says. His hair is beginning to dry. He looks sleepy. I start to feel sleepy, too. It gets dark earlier in the fall.

"Are you going home after this?" I ask. I glance at him to see how he feels about it.

He thinks, still chewing. "I'd better," he says.

"What about the dog?"

"He'd better come home, too."

"Won't that upset your dog?"

"He is my dog."

"I thought you said he wasn't!"

"Well, not when he's acting like *that*, he's not my dog." We laugh. He chews again and looks just like any kid, any normal kid who has been having a sad time and now feels better.

I ask him, "So you aren't afraid anymore?"

He looks at me and shakes his head no. He says, "I won't be afraid anymore."

"You don't just have to say that because you think it's what I want to hear."

"No," he says, "I don't."

He finishes his bread. I reach over and touch his rosy ear. He giggles. The dog gets up and walks to the hall. It stops and looks back.

I walk them to my front door. My old front door. I open it and let them out onto the porch. I call goodbye and close the door. If they're going to vanish I don't want to see it.

After they're gone I feel awake again. I walk out to the garage and begin piling everything I see into garbage bags or the sagging boxes that have been sitting for years. When they're full, I drag them from the cold dark of the garage down to the curb. I hardly pause to pick up the things I drop, leaning and scooping them up on my next trip in or out.

Back inside the house I pack the linen closet. The only boxes left are small and I stuff them with washcloths, towels, and sheets. When I bought these things I was a different woman, somewhat hard and narrow, dreams lined up like clothes on hangers. The boxes are too full, but I tape the flaps shut over the humps and shove them into the bedroom across the hall. I don't want any of it, but I suspect—I know—that at some point I will. Or someone will.

The Ruins

When you talked, your words were white, bleached branches, dusty chalk stones, bleak heat in a desolate wasteland. You delivered them lying down. You were tired, you said, but you loved me.

Looking up into my face, angling your head, half asleep, you said it. "Love you," you said, and then you closed your eyes. This was what you had become: a solitary figure on a bed of stone. I came and went, circling you, looking for things to do, then coming back again. I leaned against your stone and watched the stars appear in the sky. I talked to you. It seemed you might be listening.

If my shadow crossed the sun that shone on your face, you might open your eyes and ask, vaguely alarmed, "Is everything okay?" But before I'd answer, you'd shut your eyes again. Your words were like pebbles, kicking across the hard ground.

I don't remember when we came to live in the desert, but you liked it.

Once we lived in a little house near a river. We were very happy. When we first moved in, we laughed often. We had friends over. We walked to the river. We ate and drank and made love in different rooms.

After a while, though, you began to want, to seek, this dryness. I saw you vanishing into it, and I followed you. Out of love. Out of habit.

The desert was not disturbed by the likes of my weather. The humidity, flash floods, and storms that I represented were meaningless. That flat land sucked my moisture in through porous sands so effortlessly that silence, and your sleep, could again prevail.

Finally, I told you that I was parched, that I was going to search for some new place, a place where water might fall. You sent a lizard skittering across the rocks. The reptile blinked, puffed his chest red, and then fell motionless for hours, staring out at something else.

After that, I set out a little ways and began building near an old arroyo that looked like it would catch water if it ever rained again. I wasn't going to leave you there. I was close enough that I could see you in the distance, but far enough away that there was the chance water would come. I waved to you every so often, and even though you didn't wave back anymore, I believed that you were still watching me. I felt it was only decent that I should try to build something for us, since it looked like we'd be there awhile.

It wasn't all sand, which I considered good because there were plenty of rocks. The stone was sand-colored, with occasional beige or white variations.

First, I built a small turret and underneath, an outdoor sitting room with clever places for a garden to grow, complete with low, curved walls along which I imagined tendrils and clutches of ivy. I built a giant stone basin where I imagined a pool of clear water reflecting tall stands of snapdragon, foxglove, hollyhock. I carved whimsical, spiral windows in little stand-alone walls, the sun pouring through and making charming shapes on the path below. I would grow boxwood shrubs, and carve them into elaborate animals. I imagined them perched along the winding path, eager to greet you, like friends. As soon as there was water.

I would dam up the arroyo and make a lake. I carved a fine gazebo with fish and snails and crabs and ducks and geese twining themselves up the pillars, and thin, elegant kissing nooks inside. In front of the gazebo, I cut five satin-smooth, narrow steps leading down to the would-be water. I imagined how we would sit and watch our reflections, stretch our legs, and feed the ducks that would come with the lake.

When the first sandstorm came, I was unprepared. It was a calm, still afternoon, and then a low black cloud hurtled across the plain. I didn't have a chance. The sandstorm winds came in horizontally, strong enough to cut your head right from your body. Each grain of sand seared, bits of broken glass against the skin. I hid under one of the benches I'd carved, but sand nearly choked me, billowing in and filling all the moist places of my face: my eyes, my ears, my nose, my mouth.

When it passed, I realized that I had to build a great wall around everything I had made, to protect myself. I built the wall while the storm's fine dust lingered, inspiring me to add a good, solid box with a hinged door, like a telephone booth, to hide in during the worst of the storms.

I didn't wonder what you did during these times, out there on the plain. I could see that you wouldn't mind the storms the way I did. I thought you might even welcome them, the blind dark they pulled over the cloudless sky. I could see how that might seem better for sleeping.

Before I knew it there was a whole village. I had built small stone houses for the friends we used to have. I figured that even if they didn't want to move here with us, they might visit. Each house had a slightly different front porch, with plenty of room for vines and flowers. In the house I built for us, I carved a great table out of the largest stone I could roll in. I rubbed the surface with a bag of pebbles until it looked polished. I imagined how cool the table would feel under our leaning arms. How we'd have big glasses of water, no, pitchers of fresh water, and we would sit there, talking with each other, or with the friends who would visit.

After a while, I realized that I'd been forgetting to wave to you. But when I went back to the first garden I'd carved, the wall I built blocked the way that led to you. I decided that you were probably fine with, relieved even by, my absence, and I went back to what I was doing.

Some days, small pebbles would grow sand shadows, tiny dunes that stretched in languorous lines. Some days, sand would stream from my heels like smoke as I walked the edge of town. I should have worried more over these phenomena. I only saw them as interesting aspects of desert living. I didn't connect them to the winds that howled, sometimes until sundown, outside my booth. I couldn't comprehend their essential design for ruin.

In the village, I carved a pack of friendly dogs, as if they were running down an alley. I carved a couple of cats, too, sleeping in window sills and stretched inside houses, in places where the sun found them. I carved loaves of bread on countertops and bunches of carrots with leafy stems. I carved bowls of peas and heaps of beans. I carved corn on the cob (every kernel included, and a few strands of silk), blueberry pies, hunks of cheese, carafes for water and wine. I set some of the tables with knives and forks and napkins of stone. I carved a wicker laundry basket left beside a bed. I carved two hairpins on a table by a mirror. I carved toys scattered on the floor. I carved a room full of musical instruments in another house.

Then there was a bad stretch of sandstorms, and I spent a lot of time cooped up in my booth. I breathed sand, and spit through my shirt. Sometimes, though, it felt like the hot wind, full of those minuscule bits of stone, was packing my throat closed, trying to suffocate me. I sat on the floor of the booth and sometimes, without meaning to, I cried. This made everything worse, as the sand stuck to my eyes and face and often I would wake to the aftermath with my eyelids and lips caked shut.

After these storms, I decided to take a long walk around my creation, to see what else it needed. I was proud, anticipating seeing the work. To think that you were out there sleeping, and I had built all this! I had made miles of flat gravel into a small hamlet. I had raised something from the particles of the desert. It was impressive, I told myself. You would be impressed.

Then I noticed that all along the edges of the village, and in the garden, sand had worn my sharp edges, my careful makings, away. The sand had filled the gazebo! The fine, sleek steps were obscured by undulating waves of the stuff. The designs carved into the pillars had been pockmarked into unrecognizable shapes. Just a few blurred tails and wings remained to suggest that there was ever anything there.

The stone basin was full and smooth when I reached it. The low, curved walls I'd made were piles of tumbling rock, with no mortar to bind them. The strong winds had worn most of the spiral windows down to hard points that looked like thorns in the shadows they cast on the path.

It looked as though I had built a ruin on purpose.

In ruins there's no forgive rate. The decay begins and pursues its end relentlessly. Nothing can shore up that which has already broken, given up, given way under the heat, the sun, the sand. There was nothing I could do.

I was broken-hearted. I thought of you. I thought you might help me. There was the wall between us, though. This wall would not fall.

I decided that I would build another turret, climb it, and get your attention. Maybe you would see my frantic waving, you would rise, shake yourself, come running. Maybe you would not want to see my work destroyed; maybe you would feel compassion for me, for what I was trying to do. Maybe you would help me dig out. Maybe my catastrophe would be the thing to wake you from your slumber.

I used the tumbled-down stones of the low garden walls to build a tower. When I finished, it was crooked and rough, nothing like my earlier work. There were clear gaps, and angles that I would never have allowed.

Climbing it took a while. But once I was up there I saw all my work spread below me in varying degrees of decline. Even the little village was filling with sand, each house becoming a dune. All that I had made was vanishing.

And it was so colorless! The world I had built was the same terrible color as the rest of the desert. As bleak, as beige, as white, as hot, as airless.

I looked at the desert for what it was. Endless colorlessness. Endless scorch. Endless thirst. Endless sand. Endless stone. Endless horizon. No water was going to come. No water could exist. What I had dreamt of, what I had built, could not exist.

In the shimmering and wavy heat, my head spun, and suddenly I saw that the ruins did not exist, either. Not the things I believed I'd built, nor the remains of them. There was only the long, unequivocal, relentless desert. What I had built was mirage. There were only long rows of heaped sand. My footsteps had trod certain paths. But nothing more. No deterioration. No decay. There could be no decay, I realized, because building was not possible. I turned around again and again, delirious in my dismay.

That's when I saw you. Your great, humped figure, supine in the sand. You did not move. You had not moved since I'd last seen you. You had become utter stone. The stockpiled moments of your life, like grains of sand, had solidified around you. They lay upon you, inert, all weight. You were heft and bulk.

I decided that I would walk. I would walk over your desert, over your prone form, over sandstorms and gravel plains, through the sky without clouds, and right on out to the beckoning horizon. I took

The Ruins

my first step, and vowed to keep going until I saw drops of water trembling at the tips of every living thing.

Just then I realized that if some of it was mirage, all of it was mirage. There was no stone tower below me. I was standing in midair. I could plummet, burst open like a ripe fruit, my blood soaking sand.

I felt myself teeter.

The Girlfriend

The barbeques themselves are generally the same: pink hamburger patties on Styrofoam, wet packages of hot dogs, chicken legs, crabs. Usually chips and pickles. Sometimes there's corn. Sometimes potato salad. The girlfriend doesn't care; she eats. She tastes everything, takes coffee when it's offered.

An outsider at these family events, she is polite. Her comments are modulated, humorous, friendly. She has a gift for families, sizing them up and winning them over with swiftness and assurance. There are classic rules to follow: fathers and grandfathers get winks and vague flirty attention. Mothers are respected for what they've done, and their sons' loyalty is visibly encouraged. She flatters sisters, brothers, uncles, nephews, and nieces by remembering their food preferences.

She loves first barbeques, loves this powerful initial thrust, watching them fall for her. When she becomes a part of the family's hope, when she becomes potentially indispensable.

The conversations at the barbeques are generally the same. Typical talk. Family or politics. Sports, kids, jobs, dogs. At least once during every barbeque someone mentions something on the table that was on sale. The beef, the napkins, the tablecloth itself. She nods at this information when it comes. She understands that money matters. She knows it will matter to the family, how she reacts to money. Would she be a thrifty wife? She would.

Physically, she's desirable. She has good teeth. Her arms aren't overly hairy. She shaves her armpits and her legs. She's pretty. She's healthy. She has an appetite. She keeps her hair neat. She wears tasteful, small earrings. She laughs often. Her feet aren't that attractive, somewhat knobby and red, but she keeps her shoes on. She imagines that someday this imperfection will endear her to them.

She wins over the families' children effortlessly, looking at their toys, playing a game with them, grinning at them when they're in trouble. She knows that later their loyalty and affection for her will be noted. They will see how warm she is, how maternal. Would she be a good mother? She would.

When the girlfriend rises to remove the piles of paper plates, the serving bowls and utensils, the mothers are pleased. The girlfriend doesn't go too far. She doesn't want to seem territorial or presumptuous. At first she only clears the table, showing that she is gracious, willing, polite. She pauses, with her hands full, at the door, then bumps it open with her young, sturdy hip. Someone will be watching, she knows. A brother, a sister, a grandmother, a child. With all of her gestures, she is communicating to them how good, how perfect it could be. This match, this possible marriage.

Then, the inevitable happens.

At Joe's family barbeque, she becomes increasingly bored and uncomfortable. Joe drinks too much, becomes bossy and impatient. She spends an hour cleaning up the crab feast with Joe's sister-in-law, who complains the whole time. Joe's grandmother smokes cigarettes at the table, wears vulgar blue eye shadow and has dyed black hair. Without meaning to, the girlfriend allows what was previously a fuzzy, indistinct comment to form into hard, non-negotiable words in her mind. About the grandmother she thinks: relentless vanity. About the sister-in-law: passive-aggressive bitch.

The girlfriend rolls a newspaper around the mounds of crab, scooping gray, feathered lungs and yellow-noodled intestines, the broken shells and dismembered legs, and stuffs it all into the outside trash can. She thinks, I can't stand this. She watches Joe and thinks, he is not good enough for me.

Plastic tables on concrete next to swimming pools. Long folding tables under small tents on grass. On wooden decks, with pink-cushioned chairs. Wrought-iron tables. Beer, wine, iced tea or lemonade. She takes what is offered. She knows her limits, stays within them.

She can hardly remember her own childhood barbeques. She knows she ate ribs and called them "bones." She remembers that her younger brother always wanted diagonal cuts in his hot dogs. But this was all a long time ago, and they don't meet for dinner now. She imagines her brother in Alaska, grilling fish or some wild animal whose meat tastes like sage. A solitary act, alone by a campfire. She imagines him with a full beard and a flannel shirt. She doesn't know if her father and his wife grill. If they do, they would never use, she feels sure, paper napkins and plates depicting happy hamburgers and watermelons on legs.

Her mother, of course, is nowhere to be found.

The girlfriend has done some traveling. When there are olives on the table, she might mention the olive groves she saw in Greece. Or she might mention the dinner she accidentally ordered in France, a bowl of cow intestines. If the family is provincial, she pretends only to have read stories about olive groves, or ordering the wrong dish in France. Regardless, they listen to the anecdotes, curious. Would she be an interesting wife? She would.

Sometimes there are deviled eggs or macaroni salad.

At Alex's house they talk of baseball, car racing. Alex's brothers interrupt each other to tell her stories of their escapades. Drunken brawls. Sunburns. Money gambled. She pretends that she is not forming judgments, that she doesn't think they are foolish. She listens to the talk of sports and it falls empty around her ears.

They talk and talk at these barbeques, they talk and talk and talk.

At John's house, the men play basketball in the driveway. She sits over coffee in the kitchen with his mother and his aunt who dislike each other. The women exchange barbs, casually. The girlfriend shifts in her chair, listening to the shouts of competition outside, wondering when she can leave.

Driving to the barbeques, she is pleased. She thinks, every time, it is going to be fun. That she will have good conversations, good food. That she will be a sort of star among them, the girlfriend, coveted. Still mysterious, still desirable. She dresses carefully, making sure she looks just the right combination of sweet and sexy. She is never dressing for the boyfriend, but for the family, trying to make the family fall in love.

Her tastes are easy to satisfy. She's not a picky eater. She eats carbohydrates, sugars, meats, and vegetables. She uses condiments, chases paper napkins that get blown off the table by the wind.

Sometimes she grills for herself at her apartment, on her cheap hibachi that she keeps out on the balcony. She grills a pork chop or a chicken breast. She often leaves it on too long while she's inside fixing a salad. Its edges crisp black and are hard to cut.

There was something about each family that she could love. Their loyalty to one another. Their willingness to laugh. Their cooking or their dogs or their kids. Each she could almost imagine marrying, joining, making children and a life within, watching everyone grow and get older. But each time something would snap inside her, and the boyfriend's great flaw would be revealed. The irredeemable flaw.

Every goodbye, every family released, contained an ending of some ritual, whether it was a particularly good coleslaw, a red, white, and blue cake, or the length of the drive home.

She is polluted by the gathered history of boyfriends inside her. This one's music, that one's movies, another's love of gardening. She remembers them, regularly, in sharp increments that litter her days. If she could cobble them together: this one's tenderness as a lover, this one's capacity for social events, this one's intelligence, this one's organizational skills. If she could only collect these parts and assemble them in one body, choose the best family, and paste them into a living, breathing album.

She hates the last nights, the nights she decides never to return. She hates saying goodbye, gathering her keys, balancing plates of leftovers, the insincere "See you soon" that she calls over her shoulder.

She stops going to barbeques. She dates the men and meets them in restaurants, at movie theaters. She takes extra work on weekends so she will be too busy to make barbeques. Then, one day, she isn't busy, her current boyfriend presses her, and she agrees. A barbeque.

Everything is as she remembered. Checkered tablecloth. Pink patties, chicken legs, wet hot dogs. Macaroni salad, beer, pickles and chips. Overcooked corn on the cob. Her boyfriend looks somewhat overcooked, too, pale and bloated, something she hadn't noticed in dark restaurants and bars.

She doesn't really like most of the people at the table. And she can't pretend to notice their good qualities like she has in the past. These are arduous conversationalists. The father is mean and narrow-faced. One uncle is a loudmouth. Another a racist. The mother has taken off, her mind elsewhere while she absentmindedly places platters of food on the table.

It's not clear what the girlfriend is after at this barbeque. She does what she always does: eats, lures, chats, clears the table. She makes sure she's in their good graces, even if she doesn't like them. But at this barbeque, she's not sure that their loving her is really what she wants, and after a while, she falters. She is silent during dinner, following the mother's lead, lapsing into her own thoughts.

She doesn't want a bridal bouquet to throw to the women of this family. She doesn't want the same turkey dinner every Thanksgiving, these people across the table from her. She doesn't want to know them, inside and out. Their stubborn quirks and flaws.

Her boyfriend, she notices for the first time, talks while chewing.

She is in the kitchen, using a sponge that belongs to someone else to clean dishes that belong to someone else. She is with someone else's mother, who hums a song she doesn't know. Even the boyfriend doesn't seem familiar. She has no secret life with him that she lords over the rest of the family in her own mind. She doesn't know him at all; she's never known any of them. They are not as memorable as the food they serve. She excuses herself.

Driving south to her apartment she gets confused. She's made this trip many times but always heading home from a different direction. She tries to imagine the map beneath the wheels of her car. The linear red and white and blue lines. She can see, for a second, where 29 intersects with the highway.

All of her boyfriends have lived somewhere off this road, this direct route that leads to her apartment. These memories are on the road, disappearing in the high beams of her car. She begins to feel sick. Too much cake? Too many chips and pickles?

It is obvious, though. It is the road that makes her sick. All of the practical paths crossing and crossing again, all of the possibilities hitting the same dead end, slamming into the black expanse at the edge of her headlights. She sees the families. They line the road like ghosts. They cock their heads at her, confused. She presses the pedal, insisting that they go, be gone, insisting that she pass through them, the brightest and most loved.

She drives on and the vision fades. After, there is only the road, and the car, and the girlfriend driving home alone.

Tail

after Stacey Levine

I woke up because something was pressing against me, a hard knot on my lower back. I rolled over and felt the bed, the sheets, the quilt. Nothing. It made me think of camping, the roots and stones under the sleeping bag. I stood up and swept my arm over the mattress. Nothing. Sun poured across the bed.

Even as I bent to check the mattress, I could feel whatever it was pressing against me, in the same spot. Slowly, I reached around, hiked up my nightgown, and put my hand on my back.

There was a lump under my skin. Hard, bony, unmovable. I carried a stool into the bathroom and stood on it. I turned and lifted my nightgown and there, perfectly centered above the crack of my ass, was the lump. Sideways it looked like a little tent, as though someone were pushing a drumstick through from the other side. I stood and stared. My pale bottom and thighs, the strange thing on my back.

I got down and put the stool back in the kitchen. I looked out the window. There was a cold, hard light on the morning. The neighbor boy slammed out of his house and ran down the weedy driveway between my rental house and his. I watched him, his thin legs propelling him, and I thought, *Cancer*.

Cancer! I put my fingers in my mouth, four of them, and bit down. I was alive and whole; it was impossible. I thought about crying, or calling my mother or brother. But I didn't do those things. Instead, I just stood there, vaguely wishing there was coffee, and then I made some. Maybe I shouldn't have made coffee if I was dying of cancer, but what the hell else would I do on a Sunday morning? I couldn't go to the doctor's office. And nobody went to the emergency room for lumps, did they? What was done with lumps anyhow? Removed, dissolved? Did they usually appear overnight?

I watered the plants. I read the comics and watched a movie. Sometimes whole blocks of hours went by and I forgot about the lump, and when I remembered, I wasn't as frightened as I felt I should have been. It was backwards. I felt as though there was something wrong with me because I wasn't frightened, not because I had the growth on my back.

It was like I'd been waiting for it.

By Monday morning it had grown into a stub. Longer, thicker, more prominent. I called off work and made an appointment with a doctor. I didn't really want to go.

I sat in the cold office wearing a pale blue gown. I didn't like the doctor. He smelled like mothballs. He measured the growth on my back. He wrote 'three-inch protrusion' on my chart, felt the stub with hard fingers, pressed the skin around it.

He said, Bone spur.

He sent me for x-rays. I was facedown on a table, weighted by that heavy lead blanket, and suddenly I thought, *It's not cancer.* I was so sure I would have gotten up and left right then if it wouldn't have been so impolite.

When the doctor looked at the x-rays he shook his head. He prescribed anti-inflammatory pills, painkillers, and an anti-calcifying agent. He referred me to a spine specialist, a friend of his. He spoke as though he wished he were elsewhere, half looking at me, half looking at the wall behind me.

Finally, I said, "Look, I don't think there's really anything wrong with me."

He laughed scornfully and said, "Of course there's something wrong with you. You're growing something and unless it's a tumor or a baby, you're past the age for growing things." I took the prescription slips and thanked him but I didn't get them filled, and I didn't believe him.

After all, it didn't hurt. It grew.

My clothes didn't fit over the stub comfortably so I went to a flea market and bought a pile of those gauzy Indian print skirts with elastic waists. It was far from corporate dress but nobody ever saw me. They just breezed past my desk on their important business, nodding at me maybe, or asking for new messages. I could have had a blue face. Come to think of it, in that office we all could have had blue faces, for as much as anyone looked at anyone else. But what did I know? Maybe they had parties together, cocktail soirees or luaus. I wouldn't have gone if I'd been invited. I'm no good at small talk.

I started wearing the skirts right away, and no one said a thing.

Eventually the stub became what it obviously was—a tail. Pink and fresh-skinned, it grew long. Close to my back it was as thick as a cucumber, but the farther away it got from me, the thinner and more flexible it became, with a nice round tip, like a pencil eraser.

I called my friend Rhonda and she said, "You're kidding. A tail?"

I said, "I'm not kidding."

She said, "Why on earth would you grow a tail?"

"I don't know."

She said, "Jesus. Can't they surgically remove it or something?"

I said, "I don't think I want it removed. I don't."

She said. "Of course you do. Jesus. A tail! You have to have it removed. It's ridiculous. You can't walk around with a tail. It's not normal."

"But," I said.

"But nothing. Is it growing out of your head? Use some common sense, girl. Who's ever going to marry a girl with a tail?"

"Rhonda," I said. "Don't tell anyone."

"Don't worry," she said. "I wouldn't want to."

I slept on my side or my belly and sometimes I woke with my back aching from the effort of not rolling over. One day I realized I'd been awake for awhile, just staring at the water spots on my window, and I started to cry. Just like that. I thought, it's not cancer, it's not malignant, it won't kill me. But it's a tail and it's going to follow me forever and now nobody, anywhere, will ever really understand me. It was going to be me and this tail alone.

Because of the tail, I avoided chairs with hard backs. I had to shut doors slowly after I passed through them. In the shower, I ran the length of the tail with a soapy washcloth, as if it had always been there.

After a couple of weeks the tail became bristly. Then the bristles grew longer. At first there was a nice coat of short fur, and then that fur grew. The hair was gray, a dove-colored gray, with occasional stripes of white. I couldn't say they were even full stripes. Maybe more like streaks. Bolts of white. It was healthy-looking fur, long and soft.

The tail hung from above my ass, sort of pulling on the skin of my back. I didn't mind. It felt sexy to have it bobbing there, moving in time with my hips. Sexy in a way I'd never been. Sexy like movie stars or naturally beautiful women, a sexiness I couldn't help. I didn't try to move the tail, but once or twice when I was sitting down to eat I saw the tip come into sight and then whip away. I pretended not to notice. How could it move without me?

It followed me around the apartment, swishing out from beneath my skirt or nightie as I walked. It dragged on the floor and slammed into doorjambs if I turned a corner too fast. This didn't hurt so much, but those knocks thumped all the way up my spine, all the way up my neck, my head buzzing for an hour afterwards.

The tail cleaned the floors of my house like a dust mop. Furls of dust and hair, bits of plastic and string and lint and fingernail clippings. Soon it needed grooming. I bought a hairbrush with a wooden back and rounded bristles. I combed the fur until it was clean again, shiny and without mats.

When I went out, I looped the tail under my skirt with a wide piece of burgundy-colored ribbon.

Still, it was a problem at work. I couldn't sit comfortably in my chair. I leaned forward all day, my back knotted and stiff.

Sometimes the tail slipped free after I sat too long. One day on my way to the copier I passed Jean Tertlebaum's desk and felt it come loose. It fell on the floor behind me with a whump. Jean looked up and I kept going. The next day she leaned over my counter and asked me conspiratorially if I'd brought my dog to work. I told her I didn't have a dog. She looked at me, irritated, and then said, "You ought to know by now who to trust around here."

I did know who to trust around there and that was nobody. I didn't trust her, not one bit, but I wasn't going to lie, either. Later I thought it was stupid of me not to just show her. The tail just showed up, after all; it's not something shameful that I went out and bought, or a habit I ought to hide. Why should she have cared? But then I thought of Rhonda, and how she hadn't called since I told her about the tail, and I was glad I'd kept my mouth shut.

All day, five days a week, I took phone calls for the brokers in their hive of offices. I directed their calls down the halls and corridors. I buzzed people in and out. I took messages, took calls, took rudeness. Suddenly, I was bored. I no longer dreamt that someone would notice how efficient I was, that someone might call one day to find out about the pleasant and useful woman at the front desk. I realized how silly it was to think that anyone would ever call down and say that.

I saved my grooming for work. The fur was quite thick by now. I picked things out and put them in a small pile on my desk next to my pink message pad. I combed the longest hairs and made them pliable. Some days, with a little spit, I wrapped lengths of fur around my index finger to make curls. The time at work passed much more quickly.

I didn't always feel like answering the phone. I began missing calls.

When I did answer, I spoke the name of the firm, waited until the caller said who they wanted (Never me. Why would they want me?), and sent them on through. Often, all the little lights lit up at once and I didn't hurry. I went one by one. They could wait or hang up. I didn't care.

One day, at the rush time for phone calls, I'd left my tail curled on the desk while I handled the lines. There was a tricky knot that I was picking loose with a paper clip.

It was a moment before I realized Mr. Lee, the boss, was in front of my desk and staring at my tail, which almost entirely obscured the desk calendar blotter. His cologne was so strong that I coughed.

He said incredulously, "Is that an animal you've brought to work, miss?"

I said, "This is my tail." It was the first time I'd said it aloud and I could feel the blush all over my face.

He lifted his upper lip in displeasure and said, "Don't joke with me. Animals are not permitted at work. This is a place of business."

"You don't understand. I said, this is *my* tail." I stared at his blotchy cheeks and nose. I realized I hated him. Not only him, but myself when I was there. Hated the place, hated the phones, hated the urgency everyone pretended was real.

I stood up and let the tail slide off the desk. It swung out behind me, rustling to the back of my skirt. I gathered the few belongings on my desk: a miniature African violet, my purse, a couple of pens.

"This is a stupid job," I said to him as I passed, surprising myself.

I walked across the floor to the elevator, pressed the *down* button, and felt my tail swishing behind me like an angry cat's. I could feel him staring at me. Jerk, jerk, jerk! I thought. That's when it happened. My tail lifted all by itself and whapped down hard on the ground, once, twice, three times. The elevator door opened and I got on. I turned and in a single motion lifted my tail with one hand, like the train on a gown, and pulled it in after me. Elegant tail!

I stopped wearing it doubled up under my skirt. I wore it free, hanging or flapping or dragging behind me everywhere I went. In the grocery store, at the bank, around the neighborhood. I worked at learning to lift and move it, but it wasn't like arms or legs. It seemed to have an independent sense of momentum, or maybe it was too new. Anyhow, I didn't have much control.

People thought it was a costume tail. Sometimes they mentioned it while I checked out with my groceries. Asked me if I was in a play, if I was going to a party. I told them, it's my tail. One time a woman with two children and a grocery cart full of toilet paper and frozen tater tots stared hard at me and my tail and then moved her kids and cart into another line. It embarrassed me that she would react like that, as if I were contagious or beastly or wrong. I didn't know what to do. I stood and stared at the magazines on the rack in front of me and suddenly I felt the tail swinging behind me, high and indignant.

I called my mother in Florida and told her, "I've grown a tail." She didn't take it so well, but I tried to explain. "I can't help it, Mom. Yes, I went to the doctor. No, he can't do anything. No, he can't."

My brother Michael called to confirm the news. I told him, "Yes, it's true." I said, "Do you know what? It's kind of pretty. Really. It's not all bad."

He said, "No? Well, I goddamn better not grow one. I'm telling you right now." Then he hung up.

My mother called back a week later and said, "Having a tail, darling, is not as glamorous as you might think."

I said, "I know that, Mom."

At night, I wrapped the tail around me. Sleeping on my side I curled it up and over. I dug my fingers into the loose knots and slept holding it. Or it holding me. There were days I thought my tail was the most beautiful thing I'd ever seen. That it was more beautiful, by far, than the rest of me. Days like these, the tail was everything. It seemed a force of its own, beyond me. It grew from me, it used my body to travel, but somehow its beauty was aside from me, or maybe merely included me. I couldn't decide if I should take credit for it. But it did belong to me, and if it belonged to me, then did that mean I was beautiful, that I was somehow special? After all the years of unremarkable living, did that mean I'd become remarkable?

But there were other days, bad days, when I barely lifted it over doorsteps and puddles. I dragged it because it was heavy, because it was what made me different. These days I thought it only made me uglier than I'd already been.

People in the neighborhood began noticing more often. I heard them whispering. They no longer spoke directly to me, only about me.

One day my landlord, who lives in the building next door, called out to me as I passed. He was painting the wrought-iron railing.

"That ain't no costume tail, now is it."

I stopped and said, "No, no, it certainly isn't."

He took a big breath, puffing out his belly, and said, "A tail. That's sure interesting. Now I may just be an old-fashioned guy, but I don't know. I'm not sure it's right for people to go around flashing their tails as if they're something to be proud of."

I said, "I don't know that many people who have tails at all, Mr. Whitsun, or I'd have a better-formed idea of how they carry themselves."

He frowned at me and I stared right back at him until he turned and began painting.

This kind of conversation made me nervous. It was getting time for me to work; I was beginning to need the money, and there's Mr. Whitsun acting as if there's some code of behavior regarding tails. Things were looking bad.

I watched people walk, two-legged, non-tailed people. They strolled through the park, jumped over curbs. They ran after their dogs, light, upright, clean-moving on their legs. Nothing snagged on tree roots or got caught in grates. Sometimes I was jealous. I thought, They make living look easy.

I neglected the tail for a while and it got so thick and wide it was almost as heavy as me. I could barely lift it. It dragged everywhere. Mud-caked and hardened into a crust along the bottom, it took almost all of my strength leaning against it to make it move. Worse, it began to smell. It hung outside my bed, too heavy to curl over me. I felt sorry every time I looked at it.

There was a laundromat around the corner from my apartment with benches out front. I began spending my days on the benches (it took almost thirty minutes to drag my tail down there), and I filled my time watching people walk past. This made me feel worse. The people in my neighborhood were bent and pulled and had knotted faces, like old ropes. They argued with one another and frowned over the weather. I didn't want to be like them, living their lives, but I didn't want to be like me either.

Then one night I dreamt that my tail fell off. I was walking up a steep staircase and suddenly it dropped away from me. I almost fell forward from feeling so light. It slid away, down the staircase, without me. A hole like a tomb grew inside me.

The next night I dreamt that I was sitting in a chair,

interviewing for a job, when the tail fell and hit the floor with a dead thump. I said to the lady who was asking me questions, I'll have to bury that, and as soon as I said it I began to cry.

I woke from these dreams sweating and frightened. I didn't know what any of it meant.

My mother called. She said, "Still have the tail, Miss Mouse?"

"No, Mom," I said. "I took it off and hung it up in the closet. You can borrow it for Halloween."

She was silent on the other end of the phone and then she said, "You have no idea how hard this is for me."

I dreamt the tail was on a long kitchen table behind me. It was stretched the length of the wood and I was alone, waiting. A man in a donkey mask entered the room. He spoke to me, but the mask garbled his words. He lifted a knife off the counter behind him and before I could speak he chopped off my tail. Blood poured out of me and from the stump on the table. I was screaming.

I woke up frantic. I put both hands on my tail. It was there, hanging to the floor beside me. I felt terrible then, terrible that I hadn't been combing it or cleaning it or even treating it like it belonged to me. Poor old tail, stinking like that in the first light of day.

I got out of bed and dragged it to the bathroom. Sun was streaming in through the window and across the tub and it caught the sprinkles of water as the tub filled, forming little hair-like splashes of light. I heaved my tail over the edge and felt the water fill up around it. The water immediately turned brown and muddy, so I filled the tub and emptied it a couple of times before I even got out the shampoo. But when it was time, and the water was reasonably clean, I started working on that tail, starting at the tip and moving all the way up to my ass. I scrubbed and scrubbed and dug my fingernails in and scratched out all that was lodged and wedged and matted. The end of the tail, once it was clean, even floated.

Once I'd finished scrubbing every inch, I rinsed twice, put in some detangler, and rinsed again. I used three towels to dry it and then walked out to the balcony. The sun was shining full and I sat down on the deck, leaning against the building. I pulled the tail into my lap, where it lay drying. I thought about how it would be fluffy and full when it was done. I absentmindedly petted it while I sat there. After a while I dozed off.

When I woke up, I found my tail had dried, and not only that, it had curled itself up around my shoulders. I leaned into it, running the fur through my fingers, and I thought about who would hire a woman with a tail that she refused to hide.

Photographing the Boys

I've been supporting myself on odd portrait jobs this winter. It's easy enough work, but it gets on my nerves the way the subjects want so badly to be breathtaking, unusual, gorgeous.

It's all I have, though, so when Dane calls one day and says, I've got one for you, I tell him, Okay, and I write down the place and time as he reads them to me. When I arrive, they're already there, wearing old-fashioned clothes and clowning around.

They have names. They've told them to me; there's a Sam and a Lewis, there's an Alan and maybe a Lee, but they're jostling each other and telling jokes, clamoring for my attention and smiling, so that I can't keep them straight.

They're noisy in the winter woods, their voices hard against the trickling of the snowbound stream behind us.

After a while I say, "All right, guys. Line up how you want."

They fix their caps or hike their pants up higher and some of them lean and wrap an arm around another and I look through the lens as they fall still, waiting for me to photograph them, and that's when my hands start shaking so hard their faces blur.

Because on the right side stands Death in a buttoned coat and a perfectly fitted hat and beside him, arms clasped round him, is Charm in a black stocking cap. Embracing Charm on the other side is Youth, slender and long-limbed. They both lean heavily on Death, and I can see the connection between all of them.

Want is in the middle, alone and hatless.

There is a space between Want and Pride, a snow-white space leading to the forest beyond, and in this tree-trunked wasteland stands Sorrow, half smiling, an arm uncertainly raised to touch Pride's shoulder. Charm belches. Youth thumps him on the head, and smiles break across the line like ice cracking a river. I feel each grin splitting me open and they're waiting for me, holding themselves more stiffly, trying not to laugh, but I can't trust my voice so I turn the camera, snapping the shutter, and finally I swallow and say, "Okay, whatever's next."

They don't consult one another. They had this planned. Want, Charm, and Youth fall to their knees and brace themselves while Death and Pride carefully kneel astride their flat backs. Tall, skinny Sorrow, an odd size for the job, climbs to the top of them all. Without shifting my eye from the viewfinder for even a moment, not wanting to break the spell, I watch them raise their heads from their necks to look at me, awkward turtles lined up for the sun, faces bright and sweet in the snow light.

They seem so simple, but I know whose neatly buttoned jacket holds the heart of them, whose strong back will carry them away. I zoom in on Death and he is not smiling, not grim, not threatening; he is only balancing his load, his hair combed and neat, waiting to be photographed. I shoot his lips. I shoot Want's hands in the snow. I shoot Youth's red cheek.

Sorrow begins to move. Slowly, carefully, he turns so that he is kneeling sideways across the backs of Death and Pride. They wince under his shifting weight. While I watch, snapping the shutter, Sorrow raises a leg into the air behind him, an awkward, girly pose. Pride lets out a grunt of pain and crumples, taking all of them with him. Sorrow falls, laughing, into the jumble of arms and legs beneath him and I shoot the rest of the roll, knowing these will be the ones they desire the most. I hold on for a moment after the film is shot, watching them through the lens. Pride is mad, complaining that his back is hurt. Without taking his eyes off me, Want lifts a handful of snow to his mouth and tastes.

What Raggedy Ann Said

At the end of the bed, in the dark, the glittering black eyes stare at us. I feel the bear beside me shudder.

He whispers, "They're going to hate me."

"No, no," I say. "Everyone gets a turn; you'll see. They know how it is."

The little bear turns on his side and snuggles closer. "Not me," he whispers. "No one likes me. No one has ever liked me."

I can feel him shivering under the covers. On the shelves at the end of the bed everyone sits neatly in rows, propped against one another, some with legs dangling, some slumped in sleep. The ones who are awake stare resentfully. Raggedy Ann is sleeping at my left side, where she always sleeps. Her arm is flopped lazily over her eyes.

I wake Raggedy Ann. I whisper in her ear the problem we're

having. She sits up and looks at the shelves.

She says, "No one minds getting bumped back a night for the sake of the new bear, do they?" The animals on the shelves rustle and murmur.

The red dog with cheap carnival-prize fur says, "It was supposed to be my night."

"Tomorrow will be your night." Raggedy sighs. "You know, I remember when a certain dog got fished out of the garbage can. It would surprise me very much if he wasn't nice to the others who are scared like he was."

The red dog puts a paw over his eyes. "Oh!" he says.

Raggedy stares at the animals. After a moment she says, "All you have to do in this life is love and be loved. That's it, the most important thing any of you can do. Please." She lifts her dress up so that her *I love you* heart shows. "I'm wearing this so that you can always remember. How would you feel if I forgot?"

We lie back down and Raggedy takes the bear in her arms. "I don't know what's gotten into them," she whispers.

Raggedy and I stay up late, listening to my parents' phone call fights. My face is on top of hers. She is wet through from my tears.

"It's all you can do," she says for the hundredth time. "You can't make them happy. All you can do is love them."

I put my hand on her little fabric red-ink heart.

"But," I say.

"But nothing," she says.

The phone rings again. I lean over Raggedy and put my ear up to the wall. The cool painted surface feels good on my hot face. My mother's voice grows louder.

"Goddamn you! Goddamn you! You son of a bitch!"

Raggedy's cotton mitten pulls at my shoulder. "Come on," she says. "Come on."

We hear the phone as it slams against the other side of the wall. The phone bells ring and then there is silence and sobbing.

I stuff Raggedy's hair into my mouth. Everyone on the shelves wakes up, murmuring, their voices frightened.

"What is it? What is it?" they ask.

"Let's go get them," Raggedy Ann says. "Let's bring everyone to bed. Everyone needs some love tonight."

When I enter middle school, there is an error. I am signed up for two classes at the same time. I don't want to bother anyone, so I go to both of them, alternating. Raggedy and I talk it over. We agree it is best to give each equal time, just like we do at home, even if I do like science more than flute.

When a Caterpillar Exploration Field Trip for science is announced and I can't look at a calendar right away to see if it falls on a science day or not, I am terribly worried. Luckily, it does fall on a science day. All afternoon I am outside in the sun with the other children, looking up into the branches of dogwood trees. I love the trees, the other children, my teacher. I love them all, and I love them more than flute.

I stop attending flute class, but I don't tell Raggedy Ann because I'm sure she will worry about the flute teacher's feelings. I don't like him as much as my science teacher. In fact, I don't like the flute teacher at all. He's always mad.

Mid-quarter, when the teachers report my absences as truancy, my mother is called in and there's a meeting. Everyone is frowning. When I explain my method of attendance, their expressions change to alarm. The vice principal asks, "Why didn't you tell us?"

I answer, "I didn't want to bother anyone."

After a silence, my science teacher laughs and winks at me. "Case closed," she says to the flute teacher. "Science wins."

On the way home my mother touches my hand as though I'm someone she's just met.

Most mornings, Raggedy sleeps in. After I get up, I tuck her back in with the sheet folded carefully under her chin. "Love you, love you."

I don't take Raggedy when I leave for college. By then she is in the pile with all the others, at the back of the closet in my mother's house.

For years, there is only a blank creature with beige fur that someone gave me when I left a job. The bear lives in my closet, silent and stuffed. I move often, looking for a better job, better sex, a better life. I don't have the heart to put the bear in a bag of garbage, so he comes with me.

After the second divorce, though, I get rid of everything. Without flinching, I put the bear in a Goodwill donation bag, his head under a pile of old sweaters and emptied photo frames.

My mother is moving and this time she's getting rid of the storage bin full of our childhood stuff.

She calls and says, "I have all your dolls. What should I do with them? Most have mildewed. I could send them to you."

"No," I say.

"Should I throw them out?"

"Not Raggedy," I say. "Send Raggedy Ann."

A week later the padded envelope arrives. I tear it open. Inside is Raggedy's head and a piece of fabric torn from her chest that says, in a red-ink heart, *I love you*. Both the head and the torn fabric are in a Ziploc freezer bag.

I call my mother. "Where is the rest of her?"

"She was all stuffing and dry rot. I figured I'd just send the parts that you'd want the most. I threw out the rest. Nothing much anyway. One leg was already gone."

I keep Raggedy in her plastic bag inside the closet, resting atop a stack of old journals.

One day I get her down.

"Listen," I say.

Her blank expression stares at me through the plastic. I take her out of the bag. Her cotton face is stained and pale, with circles of dried glue where her eyes used to be. The patch of her chest with the heart is frayed along all edges, the top of the heart torn.

"All this about love," I say. "I have to talk to you."

The head sits on the bag. She is, despite her missing arms and legs and torso, smaller than I remembered.

"About love," I say. "I've got a problem. I love everyone. I love them all so much. I can't stop. I can see everyone's point of view. I can see how they all feel and I'm sorry for them, or happy, or angry for them. I'm in love with everyone. I fall in love every day. It's too much, don't you see? You're wrong. You and your red-ink heart. You're wrong about love. You can't love everyone. It's impossible. It's bad for you. Look at you. Look what's happened to you."

Her neck, where it has been dismembered, is folded up toward her face. Inside her head are thick wads of cotton stuffing. It is good-quality stuffing. I smooth her neck folds down while I talk. The stains I've left on her over the years are brown at the edges. She is bald. Her soft, red mop of hair is gone. The back of her head is umblemished, white.

"I need you to talk to me," I say. "You and all this love. It's your fault. Can't you give me some advice? There's no room for you in this world. Nobody likes your concept of love anymore. Love is completely outdated. Can't you tell me what to do?"

The stained face is limp.

"Goddamn you," I shout. "It's not equal sharing, equal love! You were wrong, you hear me! Stop insisting! You can't love everybody the same! Everyone is not deserving of love! You can't expect everyone to love you back!"

The red of her triangle nose and the perfect oval of her lips have faded to orange. I pinch the fabric of her heart with two fingers and shake it in front of her.

"Shut up about love! I don't love you anymore!"

I throw the heart on her face. It lands, covering one circle of lost-eye glue.

"You!" I say. "Who could love an old whore like you?"

Talk of Dreams

"She's had another dream," the gardener said, sinking into the wooden chair. It creaked under him and the cook winced. She wondered if it would, one day, give way beneath him. It was a worry to her. What would she say to him if he were in an undignified heap on the floor? "This time it was about an antelope."

"Why do you think—" the cook asked suddenly. "Why do you think she tells you her dreams?" She hated talk of dreams. Wasn't there a way to another topic? She'd gladly talk about another topic. People, no matter what kind of house, would talk of dreams, they would. She'd heard all kinds of dreams, those of the milkmen and butchers, maids and butlers and gardeners, plenty of gardeners, but never the mistress or master. Everybody else came into the kitchen like it was their own and spilled their messy dreams on her table while she kneaded dough. As if it was at all proper to speak of such private things. And now the mistress had told the gardener her dream, and the gardener was here in her kitchen. She could see he was going to tell her the dream.

"Eh?" Lost in his own thoughts, he missed her tone. She liked the gardener, she did. More than she meant to. She liked the mistress, too, and that was a surprise, to be sure. And what was the good of all this liking? The mistress hardly ate anymore, so how long would a cook be needed?

"It was a strange one," he said. "It's got me thinking."

"All dreams are strange." The cook said it flatly, but he didn't notice.

"In this one, she's at the grocer's, paying. But when she looks over . . ." He was going to act it out for her, she realized. He was looking over his shoulder as if he was paying a cashier and peering at something in a far corner. The cook wondered if this was the way the mistress had told it to him. If she had sat up in bed and acted it out for him. The gardener gestured toward the huge black stove. "Over by the door, she sees an antelope. Big as life."

"How does she know what one looks like? I wouldn't know. I don't know."

The gardener paused and blinked from the wall to the cook. "What?" he said. "Oh, when she was a young woman . . . when we were all young," the gardener laughed, "the judge took her on a trip out there to the prairie lands. He was settling some dispute for a family that had once lived here and pioneered out there. A fine man, the judge. But anyways, that's got nothing to do with the dream. So she sees an antelope in a grocery store." He waved his hand in the air, dismissing the need for a reason for the antelope. The chair creaked beneath him.

"Well," the cook said. "An antelope in the grocery store." She couldn't pretend to be impressed. The story about the West was interesting; why couldn't they talk about that?

"Yes." Undaunted, the gardener went on. "But after a moment, she realized that people in line were ordering antelope. They were ordering hunks of meat from that particular animal. Still alive, mind you!"

The cook let out a thin and sudden hiss, stopping him. She said, "I'll be damned if all I'm cooking is fish. I'll be damned if it's to come to that."

He stared at her in genuine surprise, as if he hadn't suspected she was not as caught up in his tale as he was.

"I'm just stating," she said, sniffing, "that the butcher's delivery will be here this afternoon, and there's lamb as well as beef coming."

"It's a dream," he said, peering at her from beneath his gray brows. "That's all. Nobody said anything about changing meals." He shifted his feet on the floor, and the sound of his heavy boots filled the room. He sighed and frowned at her, his head cocked.

She didn't understand the first thing about him. Why, for example, he would look at her so plainly? And why talk of dreams at all, much less the dreams of their mistress? She stood up and crossed to the icebox. She opened it and took out the butter.

The gardener said, "I don't mention every dream she tells me, but I thought this one interesting. I try to figure them out sometimes, so as to better help her."

"Help her." She repeated this involuntarily, wondering as she always did at the man's loyalty. What was the mistress to him, after all? Wasn't he only her gardener? Did he not pick the June bugs from her roses and pinch them dead? Wasn't he the one who spread cow manure under the vegetable beds? Pinned hollyhocks to the porch rail? And what on earth did he, a practical man, see in a woman who lay in bed all day, coughing and wheezing and almost too weak to lift a spoonful of poached egg?

He'd been here for years and she had not, she supposed. She'd had her position in the north end of town, with the politician's family. And of course, all the places before. She ought to get the bread baking. Would he sit here all morning?

The gardener stared out the window and continued. "So, the animal is lying there in a pool of blood. There's a young boy in the store, and he's the one who makes his way over, and he bends and hacks at it with a big knife. Then he tosses the meat in a paper bag and hands it to the customer." The gardener pauses, then shudders, saying, "She said the bag was soaked with blood. And dripping. So she can't stand it, see? She rushes over and kneels next to the animal. She puts her arms around its neck."

"In the blood?"

"What?"

"She kneels right down in that pool of blood? I shouldn't think she'd want to do that." The cook looked away from the gardener and tisked. She crossed the room to take down the tin of flour.

He was silent and when she turned back to look at him, he was staring at her. His eyes, blue and bright, made him seem younger than he was.

Impatiently she asked, "What is it?"

"You don't dream, do you?"

"I do so."

"No, you don't, or you'd know there's a strange sense of things. Dreams blur details. Or make them sharper." The gardener cleared his throat. He wiped his face on a crumpled handkerchief. "I won't keep you from your baking any longer." He stood heavily, and turned to leave.

"I dream," she said, not wanting him to leave annoyed with her. "I dream about a house I'd buy."

He turned back to her, shaking his large head. "That's *day*dream," he said. "That's not the same."

She took her hands off the flour tin and turned to the window. She opened it wide, and after staring at the dead insects caught on the sill, leaned for her rag and wiped the surface clean. Underneath the window, his peonies were heavy-headed and drooping. Their blown heads were crawling with ants.

"Maybe I don't dream," she said, turning back. "I'm sorry I interrupted you." She pulled out a chair, sat, and folded her hands in her lap. She did not want him going off angry with her. She couldn't bear it, him tending his paths, thinking her stupid.

He pursed his thick lips. He sat down and she heard the chair creak. He shook his head and looked into her face. She glanced away, and nodded for him to go on. He waited a moment longer, until she looked back at him, and when she did, he started again. "So, she sits beside the antelope. She touches the fur and it's bristled, stiff with blood. And even though she is sitting there, next to the antelope, the boy still comes to cut away the meat. She looks right into the antelope's eyes, and it shudders when the boy cuts through its hide and tears away a chunk of its haunch. She said the eyes were like gates into something immense." The gardener's face reddened, not from embarrassment, she realized with alarm, but emotion. He wiped his face with his handkerchief again and added, "A dying animal being comforted by a dying woman . . ." He broke off.

The cook heard a buzzing outside the window.

The gardener cleared his throat and continued. "She asked the antelope what she could do for him."

The cook looked down at the table, at a wide burn mark, from before she'd come to work there. She'd never left a burn mark in her life. It was shaped like a crescent. The tables were not hers to burn, she'd been told often enough. But someone had burned it. Ruined it. And now, here she was, left to stare at it.

The kitchen seemed terribly hot suddenly, and she drew her hand across her forehead and thought about how she didn't want to hear any more of the antelope story. It was sad and the gardener was getting worked up over it and she didn't want to see him like that because then he wasn't the gardener anymore, he was something else, and when you had a job, you didn't know how long it would last, and it did no good getting attached to good-looking gardeners or damnably sick women who hardly ate a thing no matter how good a cook you were, and who spent their time dreaming about antelopes. It was too much. She was only the cook. She looked up at the egg basket, full of brown globes.

She didn't like dreams. She'd had the one about her brother too many times to count, sitting just like that together, on the ledge outside the mill, and there he was, fine in the sun, chatting with her about anything she wanted to talk about. She'd had that dream often enough and what good had it done her?

"The antelope doesn't want to die in the grocery store," the gardener said. "He wants her to take him home to die.

"So she takes him." The gardener was sweating. She wanted to stop the stream coming down his forehead. He wiped the drops away as he talked. "There they are, that blood on them both, his lids getting heavy over his eyes, and he's bleeding into the soil of the field where he lived his whole life, and he takes her all the way, *all the way*, into his life. He tells her of every hour, about the heartbeat of his mother and the gurgle of her guts, the thunder of the herd, about stamping across miles of sage, the taste of sagebrush and the silk dust spurting from his hooves, thunder rolling black overheard, sheets of rain, coyote stink creeping down a butte.

"She becomes his *witness*. That's how she put it. A witness to his passing. She grieves, holds the antelope, and she listens to his death talk. She bids him goodbye from this life, and next thing she knew, she was back on the grocery floor with a heavy, bloody, dead antelope in her arms. And then she woke, and she was in her bed here."

The cook thought maybe she should quit, right then and there. She didn't want to see the garden through its seasons, didn't want to take bread to the woman dying upstairs. That's what the cook would do, just leave the bread unbaked and walk out the door, along the gardener's flowered paths. She would leave and not see the peonies into their browning death. She would forego the gardener's damned late-summer hydrangeas. His late lilies.

The gardener was looking at her again with his head cocked and she didn't know what to say. Should she offer him tea, or tell him she was leaving? She was nauseous. The gardener was flushed and seemed to be waiting for her to say something, and what was it?

What was that look, grief or joy, on his face? What should she do with a look like the one he was giving her? He was just like her brother, talking to anybody, doing favors for people when he had no business doing so. Why did people have to sit in your kitchen at all? Why talk of dreams, of bloody floors? All she wanted was to make the bread.

"I don't want it," said the cook, and she heard a tremble in her voice. She could feel her eyes heating with wet. She would not have it. "I don't want it. I don't want to hear any more." Her voice was rising and the tears were coming no matter how she hated it, and she turned away from the gardener to hide them and squeaked out, "No." She reached up and plucked at the egg basket, hands shaking uncontrollably, until it jerked forward and the eggs spilled down her arms and smashed into shivering jelly and yellow slabs on the floor.

"Anna!" the gardener gasped. "Anna, I'm sorry. Oh, I'm sorry to have upset you so. I didn't mean to. Let me help you." He knelt at her feet, his huge hands scrabbling at the broken eggs and shells, scooping them into his wide palms, while she stood over him, tears streaming hot. She stared at his head, noticed the gray streaks in his hair and heard him say her name again as he looked up with sorrowful eyes. "Anna," she heard him say. "Anna."

Just then, the warbling voice of their mistress called to them. They heard it drift down the kitchen stairs, and the cook turned to stare up the dark ascent. The voice called again, curling down to them, sweet and small, and the cook thought she might just fall to her knees, right there in the mess, and weep for not knowing what to do.

The Appeal of Chaos

When spring came, she took a saw and drove horizontal lines into the bark of the maple on the edge of her lawn. She tore up her bed of flowering hostas and left them on the dirt, leafy and withering hands. The great holes she dug in the lawn lingered like burn marks.

Since then, she's moved inside.

With her hands and her teeth and her strong arms and legs, she tears the house apart, bit by bit. She does this mostly at night. Or at least that's when I watch her. She smashes trinkets on the floor, breaks glasses in the kitchen sink. She needs bigger tools now: a crowbar, a rubber mallet, a hammer, a saw. She brings stacks of china plates into the dining room, small jade figurines, her clothes, and big steel scissors. She lines things up on the table and works her way through them. Crushing, hurling, smashing. In some places, she has used the rubber mallet to break through the wall, baring the yellow upright studs. Wires hang amid crumbling Sheetrock.

Her racket wakes me up. Sometimes I can hear her grunting.

I first met her during a snowfall in January, before she began destroying her house. Our driveway runs along her backyard and she was out one morning, in boots and a robe, tramping hard circles on the snow, rings that intersected. I spoke to her and she looked at me, startled. She was so bright and alive that I couldn't make myself walk to my car, away from her. We stood a moment and then I said, "Nice design you've got there." She frowned slightly, looked down at the snow, and then at me.

"I can't stand illusion," she said. "The idea that things are solid, it's such a lie. Snow is the worst." Her voice was deep and graveled, not at all what I'd expected.

The plane of my yard stretched to my right, a sheath of snow, looking as permanent and smooth as the surface of rock. I thought about how much everyone loves the way snow looks before it melts and how they complain for weeks about the gray mess left behind. I walked out into it, and began trudging circles just like she had done.

She went back to her own circles and the only sound was the squeak of my shoes and her boots. My nose was cold and my fingers were stiff on the handle of my briefcase. When I looked up to say goodbye, I realized that she'd already gone inside, that she'd been gone for some time.

In the light of the bare bulbs she's left jutting from the ceiling, her hair stands out in wild golden-brown knots. She wears torn clothing that hangs from her body. The clothes flutter in shreds from her shoulders, a knotted robe tie cinching them at her waist. Sometimes I see a pink nipple. Sometimes both breasts. Sometimes her pale ass or bony hips swing into view when she moves. I pretend that I am only concerned for her, that the sight of her nipples does not stir me in any way.

My girlfriend calls me back to bed. Her voice is sleepy and languid. "Come back," she says. "It's cold out there."

Some nights, when I get back in bed, I wonder what would happen if I tiptoed down the stairs and out the front door, crossed my wet grass and the sharp gravel of the neighbor's driveway. If I put my bare feet on her damp, ruined lawn. This is how I fall asleep sometimes, imagining.

When the petals from our Bradford pear reach her lawn, fluttering across the dirt holes and tall broken grass, she leaves them there. Somehow, in her yard, they look like litter.

Every night it gets warmer. I stand at the windows and watch her. I can't remember, after watching for so long, if that morning in the snow was a dream.

When my girlfriend is downstairs reading popular novels, I can hear the pages turning, as regular as a clock's ticking. Occasionally she sighs or shifts her weight in the chair. Sometimes she gets herself a snack from the kitchen. Eventually, she comes upstairs to get ready for bed.

The neighbor knifed her screens weeks ago. The pieces of wire mesh hang blowzy in the night breeze. Sometimes she stops what she is doing to angrily smack at her neck or the backs of her legs. I hear the moths and mosquitoes fluttering and buzzing against the screen in front of me.

My girlfriend is in the bathroom, washing her face with soap and a washcloth, brushing her teeth with fluoride toothpaste. I know exactly how she will dry her hands on the towel that hangs next to the sink. I know how she will tighten her robe and walk into the bedroom. How she will drop her slippers at the closet, hang her robe on the door. Downstairs in the kitchen, I know the dishes are done, the counters wiped clean, plants on the sills drinking up moonlight.

If the neighbor moves out of sight and into another room I follow her in my house, going to the nearest window opposite hers.

Sometimes, I pull up a chair. I have nowhere near her stamina. I think maybe she sleeps during the day. I don't know because I am at work. I wonder if she remembers me. I think about what is solid. I think that her house is a lie.

One night while I am watching, I hear a noise and turn to find my girlfriend in the doorway. Her arms are folded over her chest and she's looking past me and out the window.

"That's strange," she says. My heart leaps. I open my mouth to utter some explanation but she speaks first, saying, "That woman seems to be destroying her house." Without another word, she turns and walks from the room. For a second, I envy her ability to do so. I can't stop watching any more than I could explain why I have to.

The neighbor is very methodical about china. She balances a plate on a broken table leg and then, with a series of blows, tries to shatter it from its center. When the plate breaks and the pieces clatter to the floor, she grunts with satisfaction, a carnal and deep-sounding noise.

One night I am in the study watching her. She is in the kitchen, dismembering a toaster. I hear my girlfriend calling and I hurry to the bedroom.

"Get in," she says from the bed. "Get in. Stay here. I miss you." She pulls the sheet up to my chin and presses the warm pads of her fingertips against my eyelids. "Close your eyes," she says. "Go to sleep." She falls asleep again, her breath smooth across my neck. After a while, when I'm almost asleep, I hear the sounds from next door of fabric tearing. I want to get up and look, but I don't. I stay in my clean bed, with the limbs of my girlfriend heavy on me. Her breath is sweet and clear, but I feel like it is choking me. I hold my breath as long as I can and then I turn my head away from her, gasping. The sound of her steady sleep keeps me awake for hours.

By the end of June, the neighbor has destroyed almost everything inside the house. The heavier pieces of furniture she has hacked at with an axe or sawed into violent, angular designs. These hulks stand in the rooms, maimed and heavy.

Suddenly she has paint, cans and cans of it. She tries to work methodically, as with the china, lashing the walls with color, but something about the painting maddens her. She has fits. Sometimes she picks up a can of paint and slams the whole thing against the wall, again and again, until no more color spews out. I have seen her go further, even clawing at the paint with her hands, pounding the strong meat of her arms against the wall. One night she turns and faces my side of the house, blue with paint, blue smeared in her knotted hair, in wet streaks across her body. I push up from my seat and find myself in the hallway, ready to go downstairs and out through the door. In the dim hallway light, I can see pictures of my girlfriend and me on the wall, posing with our families, our friends. I grit my teeth and inch my way back to the bedroom like a robber.

I think about sending a note. I would write: You look beautiful in blue. I would write: You can have my china. I would write: You can have all the things in my house, anything. I imagine how she would chew up the note and spit it out the window at me. I imagine how she might pick up and leave if she knew I was watching.

Sometimes I think she knows I am watching. Sometimes I think, if I went down my stairs and out my front door, if I crossed my lawn to hers and entered her doorway, she would be waiting for me. Under my shoes the china would crunch and she would be sitting on a half-broken chair, waiting. She would say in her rough, disused voice, I have been waiting for you. She would nod her head in the direction of the stairs and I would follow her, stepping cautiously around the holes in the planks, careful not to fall where the banister has been chopped away. I would follow her through the upper hall and past the empty, wrecked bedrooms. I would pass a room where a dark nest of fabric and torn bedclothes lies curled in the corner like a dog. She would pull me by the arm when I slowed; she would put her calloused hand over my mouth when I spoke. Up the attic stairs she would lead me, through the empty and untouched space, and out the small window to the roof.

On the roof she would take me in her arms. I would smell her and we would kiss wildly, grind against each other. We would fall to our knees and she would begin eating me, mouthful by mouthful, biting the muscles of my cheeks. I would writhe in ecstasy against her sharp white teeth; I would reach over my head and scrabble my fingers against the rough tiles while she tore me to pieces and tossed chunks of my flesh and skin to the ruined bushes below.

I see her in the mornings, sometimes. Sleepily she wanders the house, kicking aside some broken thing. Sometimes she eats, I don't know exactly what; mostly it looks like slices of bread and occasionally some cheese. Usually she takes a bite and throws the rest out a window. I watch her move, the strong sinews and plates of muscle across her back.

I am suddenly aware of all that I am careful not to break: drinking glasses, plates, bowls, jars of jelly, book spines, my car, other people's cars, bottles of wine, bones.

I am afraid she will finish and leave.

On the nights she works in rooms on the opposite side of the house I miss her. I listen for her faint sounds, the tinkle of broken glass and the thunk of her saw into wood.

The first hot night of the year she pulls the broken chair into the middle of the dining room. The wall behind her is violent with orange, blue, and black from her earlier rages. I watch while she sits, gingerly, on the edge of the seat. She stares straight ahead. Smashed china surrounds her like broken birds. In the kitchen black cords dangle from the ceiling, the stove has been yanked from its place and stands cockeyed on the linoleum. Upstairs, all the windows are dark. She doesn't move.

My girlfriend is on the phone downstairs, in the back of the house. Her voice lifts and falls, with insincere bouts of laughter. I could recite the conversation she's having. I imagine rising. I imagine slipping noiselessly down the stairs in the dark, through the hall, out the front door that we painted deep green last summer. I imagine turning the brass knob and shutting the door behind me, crossing my cool, wet grass, her sharp gravel driveway, and walking up her lawn to her doorway. I would open what's left of the door, my hands touching the sawed gills of wood, and she would say, in her rough voice, "I've been waiting for you."

She would rise to meet me. She would place her muscled palms on my arms. She would look into my eyes and something burning behind her irises would stare out at me. We would turn, and I would follow her up the staircase, touching the sharp stubs of the banister's remains with the flat of my hand. I would follow her along the hallway, past the silent, wrecked rooms, and just once, I would reach out and touch the raised cord of her spine under her flesh. We would climb the stairs to the empty attic. I would follow the swish of her rags out the window.

On the roof, she would take my hand, our fingers all bones and knots, clenched together painfully, and we would walk to the edge. The tiles would glitter harshly in the streetlight.

I almost didn't wait for you, she would say, and the next step we took would be right off the edge, arms flailing, our bodies twisting in the dark as we passed windows, meeting her broken landscape with our whole selves.

I hear my girlfriend hang up the phone and before she can call out to me to repeat the conversation I know has occurred, I run down the stairs. I'm already out the door, halfway across the lawn, when I hear the first syllables of my name.

This Boy in History

He skitters to his left, leaps over cobblestones, crates, carts, old women and their heaps of fabric. The boy is carrying a pot. The slight clatter of the pot's lid accompanies his running steps. He ducks down narrow passages, glances blankly at the metal doors, the shimmering copper jugs and thickly woven rugs. The alleys are jammed with flat cakes, long tubes of sesame bread, oils, and bearded coffee sellers. The boy doesn't look at the food; he doesn't look at the aged and shining cobbles under his feet. He carries the pot always ahead of him, eyes flashing black, and he runs.

Once in a while, a tourist with skin like an apricot will hold up a hand to stop him, smile kindly, ask him to wait, to slow, ask to buy him a meal. He stops, shirt open over his skinny, heaving chest, and stands holding the pot as neither an invitation nor a warning, his expression unchanged. The soft woman will lift the lid, she insists, smiling as if to imply that she is willing to bear his burden, but when she looks inside the pot she shakes her head in confusion, her smile uncertain.

When this happens, the boy replaces the lid with delicacy and care, as if there were a snake inside, waiting to uncoil and strike.

He does not stay to hear the woman murmur to her friend, *but it was empty!*

He turns and runs again.

A story like this begins in the silence of a kitchen. Where the mother of this boy rarely speaks, and only does so with the plucked strings of a bickering harp. Where the father sits, dulled, thick and red and mute. Where the mother murmurs to herself the faults of the man, until his glowering eyes pin her lips shut.

Or does it begin before the father ever set eyes on the mother; does it begin in his ignorance, his youth, his willingness?

Does it begin before he ever set foot in her father's house?

Or does it begin in the coiling flame of hope that lies dead inside the mother?

The loam of the place where they live is bloody. It is soiled with hate and burned bare by the sun. No one possesses the fat of kindness to lend. Or this is what they tell themselves. This is how they behave.

The mother is of a hundred generations of the malevolent place. It began before she was born.

It began before the father was born.

It began again in them.

And what of their son?

The boy plays by himself. On the corner of the terrace, on what has not been blown away by the past forty years. He builds things with the jagged rocks he gathers, tempers them with feathers, weeds, olive leaves, his own marks in the sand. His fingers drag lines in the dirt city, and all day he works, even crouching over it to eat his bread, which he has carried out from the kitchen. He watches his shadow, moves a knee or an elbow to make his presence known to the imaginary citizens.

Sometimes in the evening, the boy climbs into a chair in the cool, dark kitchen, almost sightless after his day in the full sun. He sits in the circle of his father's morbid silence. He peers up at the dark roses of color around the man's eyes. His father no longer looks at him. The boy moves quietly, lifting a spoon to a platter on the table. No one ever stops him from doing so, but he is not invited to, either.

The boy lifts the spoon, or uses his hands. He eats quickly, quietly, slides from the chair without notice. He does not like to be near, for the slap of his mother's quick hand is sharp.

Occasionally the mother barks for the boy to help her, to wash, to leave, to come, to rise, to get out. He does not remember her speaking to him any other way.

Other days, the only voice he hears is the boom and crackling twine of loudspeakers in the distance, crooning a call to prayer. For the boy, it is only a sound marking the passage of the day, alerting him to when there will be food inside. His father does not pray.

Sometimes he watches other children from behind walls, children who play games of hostage and soldier. Children who play at hiding babies and crossing borders. Their play is all breathing and running and legs.

The boy's solitary play on the corner of the broken terrace is of stone and quiet. His heart races when he watches the other children, sees the soles of their feet, hears shouts of joyous capture, the sounds of their live-blooded play. Their hair shines with blue-sheen health. Even their arms are thicker, stronger, darker than his. His hair, when he touches it, is rough and dusty.

In a time past there was an uncle who took him out of the city. The uncle had bright white teeth and smiled. The boy watched the uncle's teeth tear bread, and flash when he talked. The uncle had been arrested, spent time in jail like so many, but unlike others, unlike the boy's father, the uncle did not speak with the curd of bitterness spoiling his voice. He spoke with white teeth, with smiles. The boy's father and uncle disagreed. But the uncle laughed. He took no offense. The mother even, the boy saw, smiled at things the uncle said. When the uncle came, the boy spent the day inside, too. In the corner, but close enough to watch.

One day the uncle came but didn't step inside the kitchen. The boy played alone in the dirt; he had formed a line of stick camels walking through a desert.

The uncle stopped, looked at the boy's work and smiled, saying, "What are these animals you've made?"

The boy pointed to his own back, got down on all fours, gestured a hump with his dirty hand.

"Camel?"

The boy nodded his head, yes.

"Have you ever been to the desert?"

The boy shook his head, no.

The uncle nodded and said, "Shall we?"

The uncle drove them in a little white car. The boy had never been in a car before. There were seats, like chairs, and music came out of holes in the doors, and the windows were made of glass and could be lifted and lowered by a crank. The boy was busy with the glass and the crank for some time when the uncle said, "No, look *through* the glass, not at the glass. Look *through* the glass."

And the boy looked through the glass and they passed billowing pink and orange spills of flowers and stone houses and street signs and long and short and wrinkled and hairy and covered faces and they were speeding in the little white car and there was no stopping or talking or anything but the moving, and the boy sat in his chair which was attached to the car, which rolled on wheels, and he sniffed the air.

The uncle stopped only once to pull up at a stand and buy a

package of dates, which he handed to the boy and said, "I suppose you like sweet things," and the boy opened the package which was sticky, and he took out a date and ate it and it was thick and sweet.

It seemed to the boy, in all that air that was coming in the cranked-down windows, that the dates tasted like nothing he'd ever eaten. They reminded him of things he didn't understand, but loved, like breezes on his face, the hooting of night birds, shadows of bugs on the ground.

When they got outside the city and the stone houses fell away to rock cliffs and the rock cliffs fell away to stones, and the stones fell away to the long roll of curving desert sand, it looked to the boy as if someone like him, only thousands of times larger, had dragged his fingers through, mounded, with thumb and palm, the heaps and valleys under the light which shone down, and used a huge finger to draw out the very road they drove on. And he and the uncle drove, in the car past the hot sand, on that road.

The uncle swept a hairy arm before the boy's eyes, encircling the desert before them, and said, "How much of man's blood can it still absorb? Should we not have expected the blood to come boiling back out one day?"

But the boy had no answer and the man did not expect one, and they drove on.

When the uncle asked if the boy would like to see a river of water, the boy was shocked to believe that there could be more.

He almost shook his head no, but resisted. There was already so much singing wind in his ears that he felt he could take no more, not a river, too, but then he felt he could not miss it, could not possibly miss seeing a river of water, too. He nodded yes at the uncle, and then again and again, wildly nodding yes, causing the wind and the car and the uncle to spin and stir and thump in his head. The uncle smiled, and reached out with long fingers and plucked a date from the box and ate it. He sang and drove and the boy ate another date slowly, thinking of the great light on the desert.

When they came to the trees, there was a little village, and stone houses not like his, not broken and exposed but old and whole, entire walls flanked with tumbling red and blue blossoms, doors brightened by pots of yellow and orange and purple. They drove on, past these houses to the river of water.

At the river, the little white car came to a stop and the uncle took the dates from the boy and set them on the backseat, nodded, and said, "Go look. It's delightful."

But the boy could not get the door open. He touched all the metal bars and the glass crank and his uncle laughed and got out and the boy watched the man's white-shirted middle as he came around and opened the door. The boy climbed out and followed his uncle down the bank to the river of water, and his uncle told him, "This is where people come to be healed. In these waters."

And the boy looked down and just then a hundred fish gleamed, flickered, and finned over the stones under the green but also clear water, and the boy gasped and clapped his hands and laughed out loud.

The uncle turned to him and looked down, and the boy thought he had done something wrong because the uncle looked so stricken, but when the uncle spoke to him, he also knelt and touched the boy's hair gently and said, "I've never heard you laugh before."

But the uncle was taken back to jail soon after, and the boy didn't see him again.

The market people are accustomed to the slapping of his sandals as he passes. More than once a day they look up too late, just catching the thin brown form slipping by, which could be mistaken for a dog's. But they know the sound of his feet hitting stone, the faint clanking of the pot's lid.

The market people do not know his name and do not ask it of one another. If they are together when the boy passes, they shake their heads, mutter a prayer, but they do not speak directly to, or of, him. He hangs in their minds only as long as a wasp in the corner of their stores, just the leggy hovering and then gone. More solid, tangible, quantifiable things require their attention.

They know that a vision of a boy that thin, running, does not bode well, and so they choose not to look. How many lost boys have they seen in these violent years? They have lost count.

If the market people did stop him, would they offer him food? Something from the simmering pots in the back of their stores, a handful of nuts from their cart? Just one or two small things to nourish such a small-skinned space of boy? But the vendors do not look up when he runs past. They know he does not steal. He does not stop long enough to steal.

No one in the market calls to him, regardless of how often they see him. Even when his sandals rot away and his feet bleed and leave prints on the stone—long, thin, snake-like crescents—even these the market people do not bother to read.

After the desert, the boy imagines another life. With sweet flowers, sweet tastes, sweet smells, sweet voices, and fish in clear-green water. With motion, and glass windows that crank up and down. With laughter. With children running and playing together. He imagines a world away from the broken terrace, away from the cold, dark kitchen, away from the corner where he sleeps at night, listening to his parents snort and sigh.

He practices his uncle's name. He practices it, and finally, says it aloud to his parents at the table one day. They turn to him, stunned to hear his voice. His mother shrugs. She shakes her head. She hisses: "He is an important man. He does not have time for babies."

But the father says, without expression, "He is dead."

The mother cries out, bends at the waist, groans as though she's been struck. The boy doesn't understand what his father has said, but watches his mother. She moans, straightens, bends again, backs slowly into a corner. Her face is red, her eyes bulging. Her lips push out and tremble. She stares at the floor.

The father, sweating, his eyes black and poisoned, shouts, slamming his fist on the table, *He's dead he's dead he's dead he's dead he's dead he's dead.*

The boy climbs down from his chair. He stands a moment longer, watching his mother. She looks up and blinks and it is as if the birds of her eyes have flown away. She stares at nothing. This frightens him and he slips out of the kitchen. He doesn't know which way the uncle went, driving the little white car. The boy tries to remember. He walks, ducking behind dusty terraces and fences and broken houses. He climbs a stone barrier, so small and light and quick that the soldiers never see him, and enters the other part of the city. He follows steps leading up the hill, and takes them running, looking around to find the way to the city's edge, where the desert will roll out flat and wide, where the blood has not yet boiled up.

Up high, the boy is sure he will be able to remember which way to go when he descends, but he becomes entangled in the buildings and houses and streets and people and lights and traffic and bushes and trees and loses all sense of the desert. He walks and walks. He sees plants as big as families spreading out over corners of the city. He sees a tree draped in rags of prayer. He sees children wearing uniforms, laughing on their way home, eating bread and meat from silver wrappers purchased at a stand. He pauses near the stand, sniffing deeply. The owner does not see him. The man scoops and stirs and spreads and rolls up the silver packets, and hands them, one after another, to the children and adults who wait in line. The boy wanders down the stone steps to the entrance of the market. There are the women in dark dresses, sitting on their bundles of green and fragrant herbs. Bright umbrellas offer them shade. They do not look at him. No one seems to notice him, a boy alone. He enters the market and is stunned by the color. Red carpets and blue bags. Rows of reflecting black glasses, showing the opposite store in every circular surface. Heaps of leather sandals. Breads laced with fruit, with seeds. Long shining rows of vegetables, red and white and yellow and orange and green. The boy wanders. In his amazement at what the market offers, he forgets that he is looking for his uncle. He drinks in the noise and color. He steps quietly across the rows of stones lining the market floor, looking and listening and smelling.

After hours, he finds himself at an opening to the outside. He blinks at the sky. He is tired. He wants to lie down. He wanders into a neighborhood. Down streets and past houses. A soldier with a gun walks toward him and the boy is frightened. He runs into a fenced yard where a dog yelps and wags his tail. The dog is under a thick-leaved plant. The boy crouches near the dog and puts his fingers through the wire of the fence that separates them. The shadow of the plant shades them both from the sun. The boy sinks to the ground and pulls his legs into the shadow. He tells the dog about his uncle. The dog listens. Licks his fingers. Sits patiently with him. Darkness falls and it is cold. The dog's fur is tan and short and sticks through the fence so the boy can touch it. The dog has brown eyes and the boy presses his cheek to the wire and to the dog's warm fur. They sleep spread against each other. After a few hours, there is the fence, and despite the warmth they share, the boy and the dog are on opposite sides. When the dog rises, the boy also rises. The dog looks at him, turns, and moves toward the building. The boy sees that the dog is limping badly.

Or does a story like this begin with a broken heart? Say the mother of this boy was once in love with a man with flashing white teeth. Say her father refused the man. Say she stopped speaking. Say her father told her she was ruined. Say, after a time, the boy's mother was given to her lover's brother. Say her father said to her, as he gave her to this brother of her lover: "You need a man who will break and tame you. I do not wish you to be disgraced. I am doing this out of love."

The boy is half-asleep. He wanders. At a stone barrier, he climbs and slips into a dusty, quiet neighborhood. He turns a corner. At the end of the street is a line of soldiers with guns. One of these soldiers orders the boy to stop. The boy freezes. The mustachioed soldier leaves the line of waiting soldiers and stalks toward the boy. The boy turns too late to run. The soldier knocks the boy to the pavement and presses the cold metal end of his gun into the boy's face.

A woman emerges from her house, weeping and screaming. She claws at the soldier's arm, crying. The soldier turns, lifts the gun from the boy's face. Shouts at the woman, shakes her off his arm. The woman is screaming down at the boy; he sees a wide black mole on her cheek. Another soldier yells at the woman. The boy scuttles away, backwards on his hands and feet, like a spider. Behind the men at the end of the street, metal tanks roll around the corner. Massive and stern. The boy runs. He can hear the woman screaming. He hears gunshots. She stops screaming. He runs. An explosion erupts behind him. The ground heaves. The boy falls to the pavement. A small breeze touches the boy's face and he scrambles to his feet. He forces his thin body through a gap in a metal fence, scraping his belly and arms, drawing deep, bloody gashes. He runs down a street where no one is moving. He keeps running, his heart thumping, his small lungs burning.

The boy runs up a hill, into a flowered, quiet, sun-strewn neighborhood. He finds a shaded, overgrown yard, and throws himself down. His mouth is thick with dirt and fear. He eats fruit from the ground, and passes out.

When he wakes, it is bright noon and his insides are liquid. He shakes and shudders against the side of a house. It feels like there is a man's fist clenching and unclenching inside him, squeezing him into brown water. He curls up on the grass. The afternoon hours pass in shadows on the ground.

He trembles and watches the light change. His body burns hollow. He is alone. He is nowhere. He is no one. He dozes off, shivering.

When he wakes, he rises again.

The boy moves down the hill. As he walks, he sees the market entrance below, where he began his day. There are the colorful umbrellas, people churning in and out of the stone archway, men with golden coffeepots, soldiers with guns. He makes his way to the entrance. He doesn't know how to ask any questions. He blinks. He sees the weeping woman again and again, the wide black mole. He blinks again. She is in his eyes. He can't close them away from her. Even now when he sees her, he doesn't know what she was saying. He doesn't know what happened to her. His chest throbs where he has torn it on the fence. He is surprised by his own blood, drying on him. He walks carefully, close to the wall, making his way down.

When he thinks of the dark kitchen, he thinks of his mother's blank gasping, the birds flying from her eyes. He thinks of the pulsing line of blue in his father's forehead, a tiny snake writhing. The woman screams inside his eyes. The black mole. His father's red-circled eyes. He does not know where to go. Where the soldiers will not be. Where the woman will not run out screaming inside his eyes.

He passes the tree of prayer rags and looks up into the mass of fabrics, faded and frayed. He crawls beneath the tree and curls his arms around his dirty knees. He watches his fingers tremble. Above him, the flags slap and flutter helplessly in the breeze. The boy shivers.

An enormous noise shakes the whole street, and again. Boom! People run past him, dragging one another, and children, by the hand, shouting. His feet are shaken from the dirt, as though he is only a bit of branch, a rock. He stands, too, and runs the way the people are running. But the people are running in all directions. He follows the men who are screaming curses, and then he is in his own neighborhood. Smoke billows in great black tongues from the houses. There are flames, and men running, soldiers running, smoke, sharp, rapid bangs. The boy crawls over the dirt and the rubble. Dirt-covered shrubs rain ash on him. He passes the house where the other children played, but it is black and burning bright. His own terrace is gone. Smoke boils out of a hole in the wall. There is a pile of rock where he played. The kitchen wall is missing. He climbs inside and stares at the wreckage, blinking and coughing in the fumes.

His father is half hidden, thick cement pressing him down.

His mother is on the floor. Her eyes are open and soft in death. She lies staring at the sky. There is blood around her head, and a great brightness over everything—the sun shining through the open roof. There is a pot on the stove and the boy stares at it. His stomach growls.

The boy slides and crouches and climbs over the heap of stone. He inches around his mother's blood-shadow to the stove. He grasps the handle of the pot and lifts. He scrabbles his way into light, just past the smashed tumble of kitchen wall. He looks back at his parents, blinks, and turns away.

Crawling again under the shrubs, he finds two broken walls tipped together, creating a little space. He waits and waits and waits until the noises stop. Darkness falls. The blood has dried into bitter red bars of ache on his chest. He peers through the slit between the walls and into the ruined street. The noises have stopped. The boy closes his eyes. The woman screams. He opens them. His stomach growls. He carefully lifts the lid on the pot. The lentils are red with tomato. He dips his fingers in and eats. He closes his eyes. The woman screams. He sees his mother's blood-shadow. He blinks.

He opens his eyes and keeps them open. He eats. He eats every bite of the lentils with his eyes open. As soon as he is finished, he struggles from the dark stone womb of walls and into the night. He drags the pot after him, and he begins to run.

Acknowledgments

Thanks to Erin McKnight for her incisive, elegant editing, and to Queen's Ferry Press for recognizing this book as a *transportive literary fiction collection.*

Thanks to Philadelphia's Interact Theatre for a performance of "The Sin Eater," and Playwrights Theater in New Jersey for a performance of "The New Plague."

For their reading, listening and succoring during the writing of this book I thank: Rebecca Brown, Mary Page Jones, Bob Jones, Cyane Tornatzky, Jake Tornatzky, Ray Rollins, Christine Rollins, Kathy Wallace, Sy Platt, Felicia Carter, Tommy Creegan, Barton Dudlick, Mary Anne Price, Renee Papaneri, Valerie Dolphin, Rich Renner, Ted Knighton, Jim Churchill-Dicks, Chris Sasser, Linda Lazar, Marilyn Keating and Debra Sachs.

Thanks to these fierce ushers standing ready: Leo Tornatzky, Noah Saterstrom, Julia Gordon, Kristen Nelson, TC Tolbert, Lisa O'Neill, Jill Brammer, Tony Dees, Laynie Browne, Timothy Dyke, Beth Laking, Annie Guthrie, Danielle Vogel, Kristi Maxwell, Samuel Ace, Jen-Marie McDonald and Deborah Poe.

Profound gratitude to the midwives of this book, The Corvid Writers: Christine Simokaitis, Dawn Paul, Selah Saterstrom, Ellen Orleans, Kirsten Rybczynski, Joan Powers, M.B. McLatchey and Susan Newell.

And for everlasting conversation, thanks to my husband, Ben Johnson, whose favorite story is "Tail."

Thanks to these journals and magazines that have previously published works from this book in either the same or slightly different forms:

"The Ruins" was published in *Superstition Review*, Issue 9, 2012

"Talk of Dreams" was published in *Flint Hills Review*, Issue 2010

"This Boy in History" was published as "The First Intifada" in *Conjunctions*, Issue # 53, *Not Even Past*

"The New Plague" was published in *Green Mountains Review*, Vol. XX, ed. Leslie Daniels

"The Sin Eater" was published in *G.W. Review*, Vol. XXV

"Tail" was published in *PMS*, Vol. 4, ed. Linda Frost

"The Sin Eater" was published by Corvid Press, Beverly 2004, ed. Dawn Paul

"What Raggedy Ann Said" was published in *Storyglossia*, #4, ed. Stephen J. McDermott

"I See Her" was published in *The Redwood Coast Review*, Vol. 5 (3), ed. Stephen Kessler

"The Boy" was published as the 1999 Philadelphia *Citypaper* Fiction Winner, ed. Lisa Zeidner

"The Boy" was published in *Washington College Magazine*, ed. Marcia Landskroener

"The Appeal of Chaos" was published in *Frisk*, Vol. 2, eds. Brandi Ramirez and Tricia Yost

"The Girlfriend" was published in *High Maintenance*, Vol. 2

"Photographing the Boys" was published by *House Taken Over*, ed. Vic Perry

About the Author

Elizabeth Frankie Rollins has received a New Jersey Prose Fellowship and a Pushcart Prize Special Mention. She authored the chapbook, *The Sin Eater*, a novel, *Origin*, and has published work in *Conjunctions*, *Drunken Boat*, *Green Mountains Review*, and *The New England Review*, among others. Also known as Madame Frankie Karamazov, she lives with her husband, artist and curator Ben Johnson, in Tucson, AZ.

About the Artists

Ben Johnson is an artist and curator, educated at the Pennsylvania Academy of the Fine Arts in Philadelphia, PA. Working within the realms of painting, sculpture, photography and film, he explores themes of the natural world and exhibits his work nationally. Johnson currently lives in Tucson, AZ with his wife, the author.

www.benjohnsonart.com

Noah Saterstrom is a visual artist and designer, educated at the Glasgow School of Art in Scotland and currently living in Tucson, AZ. In addition to his primary media of painting and drawing, he has written essays, made video works, animations, and text/image collaborations with writers.

www.noahsaterstrom.com